Praise for

M000231348

"Rick Harsch presides over a madcap yet deadly serious battle of the sexes in this tour de force of Midwest noir. The ghosts of Faulkner and Chandler range the pages as he slides between then and now. Harsch's 'Voices'—a political reporter on the crime beat; a judge who drinks for free; a witch; a one-armed sidekick; and not least Stella, a teen of startling vision whose words upend orthodoxy—all compete for flashes of the truth. Profound and unsettling, admixture of *Driftless Zone* anthropology and intimate portraiture, *Voices After Evelyn* is a riveting work of art by one of our most brilliant and inimitable writers."
— Trenton Lee Stewart, *New York Times* bestselling author of *The Secret Keepers, Flood Summer,* and *The Mysterious Benedict Society* series (all Little, Brown and Company)

"*Voices After Evelyn* marks the triumphant return of Rick Harsch, whose work I have greatly admired. This new novel—a fictionalized examination of a still-unsolved murder in 1953—is chilling, bone-honest, comic, and sorrowful. Kudos to a new press—Maintenance Ends—for bringing back Harsch's keen, indelible eye."
— Peter Orner, author of *Love and Shame and Love* (Little, Brown and Company)

"…a heartbroken, busted-up American version of the Greek chorus. Harsch brilliantly evokes each voice in its peculiar singularity, while seamlessly weaving it into a tapestry (and moving the plot forward—no mean feat). Make no mistake, even with its abundant humor, this chorus sings backup to a tragedy (a human-scale one, as well as cultural) of an America still refusing to come to terms with its noir, its cast shadow, what Carl Jung called 'the invisible saurian tail that man still drags behind him.'"

— Dorian Falco (*St. Louis Post-Dispatch*)

"Rick Harsh grew up with the stories of this homegrown mystery, of dark events in a superficially innocent time and place, of voices haunting the river bottoms and hidden coulees of the upper Mississippi. Although Harsch's own path has carried him far away, he has kept those voices close. Now he has channeled them into this memorable expression of Driftless noir. The *Voices After Evelyn* continue to haunt, and the mystery lingers."

— Curt Meine, co-editor of *The Driftless Reader*

VOICES
AFTER
EVELYN

Rick Harsch

Maintenance Ends Press ❧ Iowa City, Iowa, USA

Voices After Evelyn

Copyright © 2018 Rick Harsch

First Edition
ISBN 9781948509039
Library of Congress Control Number: 2018949860

Maintenance Ends Press, LLC
imprint of the Ice Cube Press, LLC (Est. 1991)
North Liberty, Iowa 52317
www.icecubepress.com

All rights reserved.

No portion of this book may be reproduced in any way without permission, except for brief quotations for review, or educational work, in which case the publisher shall be provided copies. The views expressed in *Voices After Evelyn* are solely those of the author, not the Ice Cube Press, LLC.

This is a work of fiction. Names, characters, businesses, places, events, locales, and incidents are either the products of the author's imagination or used in a fictitious manner. Any resemblance to actual persons, living or dead, or actual events, is purely coincidental.

The paper used in this publication meets the minimum requirements of the American National Standard for Information Sciences—Permanence of Paper for Printed Library Materials, ANSI Z39.48-1992.

Manufactured in USA

The characters in this book need never have existed, though some might claim otherwise. Most of what occurs in here may be categorized as oral history, which has the merit of being innately more fictile than The Big Lie, and more accurate by scads. To evade the truth through a trite legalism would no doubt provide me the cover this fiction bears, but I ain't calling nobody a liar, and saying none of these folk walked the earth of God's country would be the act of a coward. I think at least one guy really did work at the brewery where the beer—double-brewed (kräusened)—was made with pure water that some say came all the way from Canada, even if two characters from another of my novels figured it really came from somewhere around Wausau. —R.H.

To the Wehrs Family up on the ridge
and from the other side of the globe:

Sasikala

Arun

Bindu

Arvind

Shanthini

Marla Rothgert, the Witch

I saw Evelyn in the shower. She had the rudimentary wings of a stillborn angel.

Todd Mills, Reporter

Stay in the same place long enough, two things happen. People get so used to seeing you they look right through you. You look at them and they look back and you don't know if anything happened.

On the other hand, like an old piece of furniture you acquire a durable quality of grace. No one hurts you on purpose anymore.

I had been at the paper twenty years when the Evelyn Hartley assignment came up. We were in the conference room.

Rusty said, "Two of yoose gonna hafta dubbleup." That's the way he spoke when he thought he should.

Nobody volunteered.

"We got two bullshit ones left take but an hour or two each. There's the Hartley dig by Winona, and that broad who kept her husband in the cellar got probation we need to see if she'll talk."

Finally, our crime guy, Magnesun, spoke up.

"Todd doesn't have anything."

Rusty, who had been looking straight through me, now gave me a kindly look.

"Todd, sorry, take them both, can you?"

It was no wonder Magnesun didn't want them. They were both crime stories. At the paper there was a tradition, the crime guy got put on business and the business guy on crime and if they didn't like it there were other papers. No one knew why or how it started but that's the way it always was.

The business guy was a woman named Jackie, who sat sullenly detesting her assignment to cover outside interest in a factory that made boots.

I was the political reporter.

The assignments were fine with me. A drive up the river always does some good, but then it began to rain halfway there and I had to stand under an umbrella in 45 degrees talking to a cop who didn't want to be there and knew they weren't going to find anything.

He was a fat guy with a mole on the side of his face and like all the other cops I knew he looked like anything but a cop.

(Yet until I interviewed another cop, this guy's face would be the way I pictured cops.)

"Detective," I asked, "can you tell me what instigated this search?"

There was the rain adding texture to the loudness, and the unsteady rumblings of the bulldozers.

"A tip."

"What kind of tip?"

"Phone."

"What did they say?"

"Said Evelyn Hartley's buried in this draw."

"Just the body, or is it in something?"

"In a car."

"Can you tell me what it was about the tip that made you take it seriously?"

The answer was the make of the car, but he would tell me "no comment," even though forty years had passed since the crime.

"I'm sorry," the detective said. "That's all I can tell you."

He seemed like a nice enough guy.

I stopped him when he started to walk away.

"Detective? How long you think it'll take?"

He showed his face to the rain.

"If the rain don't get worse, maybe another hour, two at most."

So I got the hell out of the rain, drove into Winona, ate lunch and drove back out to that obscure spot that held no secrets we could decipher.

They were done and I caught the detective just as he was wrapping up.

"Nothing," he said, before I could ask.

"What do you make of the call?"

"No idea."

"They knew something the public shouldn't know, am I right?"

"After forty years, the public could know anything."

He had a point and I had a short, simple story to write that I dictated on my way back downriver, watching the clouds break into drifts of cloud as the rain eased off and the sun spat through the thinning veil.

At the office lot I checked my odometer. I had gone twenty-three miles each way, and that made me think about the radius of the crime, where the body was or might be. Ask anybody old enough to remember and it's about 50/50 they'll tell you Evelyn is buried under Losey Boulevard (named not after the film director, but his family), where it intersects State Road. That's about a mile north of Viggo Rasmussen's house, from where she was abducted. Since no part of her body was ever found, the fact that one of the shoes, possibly worn by her abductor, was found off Highway 14 southeast of town, fourteen miles from Viggo's, may not bear on the question of radius. But the search extended that far. And a few years later when Ed Gein was apprehended and his unspeakable crimes discovered, the radius went a hundred miles east to the bogs around Plainfield. Though he lived in Plainfield, Ed Gein was born in La Crosse, and he was in town the day Evelyn disappeared. About the time I came to town the radius took a bizarre flight to the Middle East when a troublesome passenger on a flight from somewhere in North Africa to Tehran claimed that she was Evelyn Hartley.

And of course, there is always the Mississippi River, downstream.

Chorus

Where's Evelyn?
Buried under Losey Boulevard where State Road slices from the river valley through a fold in the bluffs, away, Evelyn is smiling, wearing the same glasses as in her last photograph, the glasses they found on the floor by the chair, an X in the news photo, she looks younger in that photo, on the other side of puberty as if an even greater loss, Evelyn, crouched deep in the monolith of her mysterious death in the smokestack at the University—how the murderer got up there! he must have been a steeplejack—Evelyn fingering her Indian

13

bead belt, impotent talisman against the pulmonic dark moving outside the windows of the city, a mirage on the black river high over Evelyn, oscillating like a death that never surfaces, like a torn and discarded leaf of newspaper with her photograph on it, adrift, or swallowed by an eddy and never released, catfish, gars, sheepshead, carp, spoonbills, muskies like you wouldn't believe attracted to her smile, nudging her dumbly for forty incurious years, accommodating her as they do anything sunken, treasureless, vacant as the draw twenty miles upriver on the Minnesota side, where authorities bulldozed acting on a tip, news helicopter circling like a turkey vulture circling like the pigeons across the ridge, over Evelyn, under the ground, on the back seat of a car, propped friendly and well-mannered, like a girl of her type, wearing her bobby socks and her blue eyes and her fair complexion and her five feet five inches and her one-hundred and nineteen pounds, an involvate and skinflayed inamorata in Ed Gein's graveyard, Evelyn proper, her back skin incorporated into a chair, her hair on the skull of a madman dancing under the moon, illumined specter in brume, her vulva half of a matched set, not for sale, a fiend's keepsake among flesh and bone oddments, Evelyn underground in cranberry bog country without her red side-zippered pants, her white cotton blouse, her shoe, naked pushing up cottonwoods, swamp maples, tamaracks, at the end of a trail that starts with the other shoe, in the basement of Viggo's house, a pair of glasses on the floor in the living room, drag marks on the driveway, blood on the side of the house on Hoeschler Drive, blood on the side of the next house up Coulee Drive, the unmistakable bloodhound hounded odor of Evelyn leading to the absence of a car, buried twenty miles upriver, sucked under a cranberry bog, sunk in the river, a car that paused on the way south out of town at the Mormon Coulee overpass under which they found a bra and panties, chastely refusing identification yet instigating a two-mile trek through sewers all the way to Farnam Street, where Evelyn's brother emerged like a creature born inured to filth while the car escaped south out of town, the whimsy of two tennis shoes flung in succession to mock the cops who would examine them down to their Whizzer Motor Bike wear marks while the feet once in them ran and ran and ran, away from those sedentary shoes found beside Highway 14 this side of Coon Valley, which marks the limit of probability, where disappearance becomes absence, where the search should end, if they're still really searching, since you have to figure he probably wouldn't think to dump the shoes before he dumped the body, disappeared being a relative term concerning Evelyn, run off with her secret lover, a carpenter, steeplejack, biologist, spy, taken up diffident residence in Chico, California, she did it to spite her father you know, diligently reconvening the ordinary in a quotidian haunted by the spawn of invented origins and the suspicion of her double as an absence in a mirror, absence being a relative term if you agree that he dumped first the body, then the shoes, leaving her within the bounds of the Driftless Zone so that even if they never find her you can be sure she'll always be with us, grown old and bereft of emotion in Damascus, Riyadh, Aden, the cash from her sale long dispersed, her lone escape attempt foiled by a brotherhood of wealthy Muslims, the original white slavers, whose agents control Interpol in the Mideast so when Evelyn was discovered on the flight from Algiers to Teheran in 1976, 38-year-old Evelyn, they said she was mad, she was mad, apprehended her as she tried to flee through the terminal, attracting the attention of foreign correspondents, who reported the incident, so the brotherhood had to go through the whole charade of having Interpol check Evelyn's dental records, sent from La Crosse to an agent in

Teheran who of course said no, no such teeth in this mouth now wired shut, Evelyn emotionless and gone for good, silent, estranged, useless hag freezing with us in winter, thawing with us in spring, corpo as well as real, more than ether, a body that will rot with the compost of our summers, quaint mephitic evidence of the fanaticism of degradation, the futility of escape to Red Oak Ridge Island where Evelyn is a wild island harridan, a simian gray rustle in the trees, something you convince yourself you couldn't have seen, like an orange Borneo boy banished to freak show, exterminated alongside gypsy and traveling salesman and hobo, hooting from the tree tops, Evelyn taunting, refusing her death its due with a fervid autumnal optimism, rising in the death anniversary ghost stories of fall, yearly variations of conjecture with calcined aspects of fact like old man Hartley himself was in on it, up to his neck, wasn't he the one who first found her missing?, but why, why daddy?, because the little slut was pregnant, the shame of it with him a biologist and all, but if we can't abide daughtercide at least maybe he helped her escape, helped her fake it, staged it for her—he could get blood from the lab as well as he could quicklime her, her own father, a biologist who would know how to neutralize the acid of a corpse, would know from his trampings through bean fields and the ruins of farmhouses burned out by real estate moguls who bought up the land and parceled it into a housing development from which Evelyn was taken like a village baby by a rogue wolf, her father would know of an old cistern in which to practice his unthinkable, unregenerate alchemy, of course he would know, the way he would drift off in the middle of a sentence in class, the way a mention of her name would cost him the power of speech, surely the killer was one of his students, evaporating before the professor or congealing into a single hydra-suspect, remember he passed a lie detector that idiot special investigator they hired lugged into town like a mad scientist some extravagant alembic into which we pour molten all the frenzy of speculation, suspicion, fear, failure, and the will to treachery, and out of which plopped that one great turd of inutile truth…

Todd Mills

The other story was plain bizarre. Larry Browning had worked as a janitor at the brewery, and as long as anyone could remember had come to work in tattered clothes, filthy, often with bruises on his arms. As he appeared to be an idiot, scant attention was paid, though now and again someone at the brewery would ask if he needed anything or hand him a bag of used clothing. No one knew where he lived, no one much cared. There are always people like that around.

He walked to and from work.

One day the meter man for the gas company finally acted on his creeping suspicions that something was awry at the house on the corner of Fifth and Adams.

The police discovered that Larry was living in the storm cellar, one of those separate from the house with those doors that wing up aslant into the yard its only entrance, though he was connected to the house by a pneumatic tube, through which he was often fed. The pneumatic tube was part of the one that had been used for years at Herzog's hardware store, defunct as of 1977, used for the moving of mail and checks from cashier to backroom, at least that's what Larry repeated ad infinitum, with pride.

Larry was not in the basement when police arrived. But the unmistakable signs of squalid human occupancy were: a 40-watt bulb, a dank mattress, a pile of rancid clothing, a dirty plate.

Larry's wife, Adele Markham, was home and answered all police questions with laconic honesty. She was arrested and charged with spousal abuse.

Like the Hartley case forty years before it, this one made national news. The man in the cellar. The brutal, sadistic wife.

Adele Markham pled guilty, effectively quashing the investigation. She refused to speak to the press, which held the case in its teeth with the fury of a mad dog.

At sentencing, the judge excoriated the press, which had gone so overboard on a case that involved nothing but victims. Adele Markham was sentenced to a year of probation. She was not to have contact with Larry Browning, who had been removed to a public shelter.

When I knocked on the door of the house at Fifth and Adams and a neatly dressed brunette, about 5-feet-3, maybe in her 50s and just a little heavy in the gams, opened the door, I immediately thought, "Realtor: Adele Markham is selling the house." But it was Adele Markham herself I was looking at. There had never been a photo of her in the paper.

She smirked while my mind made these computations.

She held the door open but had yet to move the arm that blocked my entry.

"I don't look like a sadist?" she said, and swung into the house, inviting me to follow.

She pointed to the chair I was to sit in. The room looked like a boutique. The G.I. Bill built hundreds of houses like Adele's in La Crosse in the '40s, and about ten patterns of upholstery decorated the quaint couches and chairs in their tiny living rooms.

"Something to drink?"

"No, thank you."

"I'm having coffee."

I waited for her to get the coffee. I supposed the question I was after was why. Why lock someone in a cellar? According to the reports, none of which I had written or had anything to do with, Larry had started frequenting the cellar—as a sort of punishment, or banishment—three years before, and somehow it had become his habitat.

Adele set her coffee on a TV tray and sat in another nest of flowers the other side of it. She drew her legs, pressed chastely together in their tapering, calf-length skirt, up onto the chair, and looked in my eyes.

"Nice rain we had," she said, and now I could detect the habitual irony to her tone. I was surprised that so much life showed in her eyes.

"You *are* the reporter, aren't you?"

I suppose sometimes when you've been around too long you expect to go undetected.

"I'm sorry," I said, making an abortive, clumsy reach toward her coffee cup to cover my embarrassment. "I'm Todd Mills, yes, reporter. I'm here to interview you. Yes, it was a nice rain."

"I called because—"

"You called?"

"The paper—"

"You called the paper."

"To say I would talk now that the legal…"

"I see. I actually didn't ask how—I was given the assignment and I didn't ask how it came about."

"I don't see that it matters…"

"No, not that it matters, it's just—"

"Did you want some coffee? You looked like you were going to take mine."

"No, it was a reflex."

"So you don't want coffee, and it doesn't matter how this interview came about."

I didn't know if she was making fun of me, but there was enough flirtation in her eyes it didn't much matter.

"And it was a nice rain we had," I said.

Adele laughed a husky, delighted laugh, and then I laughed. Neither of us had expected a human moment to unpeel right out in the open of our day.

It occurred to me that if Adele was a local, as indeed she must be, she would be about the same age as Evelyn Hartley, that is, if Evelyn were alive.

"I'll tell you straight off why I want to talk now. I'm not a sadist. I'm not a sadist and I want that in the paper. Can you do that, Todd? Can you write it up so people can read in the paper that I'm not a sadist?"

"Should just be a matter of giving your version, your explanation of events."

She looked off toward the wall behind me to think that over.

I was facing the windows, with their plain shades drawn. A terrible bleakness had stolen into the room. I felt it in the pit of my stomach. I looked at Adele, who betrayed an unhappiness that seemed impossible in the face she had turned to me moments before. I realized she wasn't looking at the wall or anything on it.

Eventually she said, "That's not as simple as it sounds," and I didn't want to hear her say it.

"I was out in the rain this morning," I said, and Adele turned her attention back to me, and immediately her face brightened. I had the fleeting thought that her soul was near-sighted. "They were digging for Evelyn Hartley—"

"That's *exactly* what I was thinking about. It was on the radio. She's wasn't there, of course."

"No, she wasn't...Where do *you* think she is?"

"That's everybody's strange obsession, isn't it? Where, instead of the fact that she's gone. It's different if you knew her. Then the obsession is the fact of it."

"You knew her?"

"We were in school together, only she came from the wrong side of the tracks. All my friends hated her, but she was nice to me once, she let me copy off her on a test. Maybe she was too good to be true, but she was never stuck up, and her family wasn't really rich or anything."

"So what were you thinking?"

"About that time. In general."

"But not about where the body is."

"You know how everybody makes a point of saying they know where they were or what they were doing when Kennedy was shot—and the funny thing is, I don't, I don't know…on my back somewhere in Southern California, I suppose. But the night Evelyn was killed, that's the clearest memory of my life. I was with my boyfriend Bobby, who's dead, at the Coo Coo Club. Everybody called me Stella on account of Bobby…"

Bobby, Oct. 24, 1953

I never had a sister so I can only imagine to what extent I'd let insult pass before I'd defend whatever honor she'd accrued or had left, but I'm uncertain the threshold would arrive before she got her head swatted by a bottle, for mere words would be hard put to impel me to action. From what I've seen, women have a mysterious capacity to swallow verbal ammo and gain strength from it. Gulping the curare of expletives leaves them thirsty. Maybe I've known the wrong kind of women. Let them not distract me further, for now. My point is you can say what you want about my hypothetical sister, but not a word, a single word, against Frankie Laine, especially when he's not around to defend himself. What we owe him for injecting his sense of urgency and drama into the pulseless epiderm of our hours is incalculable. Does it matter precisely what ghostwriters or ghostriders are? Does it matter what they're doing in the sky, or how they got up there in the first place? Frankie rides rough-shod over such deliberations—his voice leaves no doubt as to their significance. He makes us want to know, at least once, for one perishable moment even, what it is to be a ghostwriter/rider, to be invested with a mission like theirs, instead of, say, being entrusted with the menial task of wiping dead bugs off windshields, ejaculating gasoline into the sterile, leaky womb of a car, replacing a flat tire with one that by the time it's in place is equally flat in your mind; that is, until Frankie Laine comes on the radio and infuses these chores with the Iliadic swell of the heroic. Homeric! like the little Irish guy says in *The Quiet Man*. Positively Homeric! Or, to take another tack, when Frankie sings, Do not forsake me oh my darlin', are you not immediately prepared to take up arms against his enemies, to risk your life to make wrong into right, etc.? You'd sooner betray Gary Cooper than Frankie. You understand before he delivers a second line how far you would fall by letting him down, for now you have inchoate in your squammies some notion as to the why of it all, beyond the plaint of good and evil, and you and Gary Cooper's woman, and everybody else within earshot, had now the courage to be good, the recklessness to ride the bottomless wave of Frankie's truth. Yes, the noonday train will bring Frank Miller, and I, and you, all of us, will be there to meet it.

I hadn't been at the Coo Coo Club an hour, Stella still hadn't returned—I'd sent her home to apply a few years of makeup, not that Ernest would ever think of kicking her out, it's just I didn't want him to feel too queasy at the sight of her—the Judge was still sober, that's how early it was; the light in the tavern was already in its crepuscular shade of temporal mockery; Nickie Turner was losing to a salesman from Eau Claire at one of the pool tables while his brother Joe strategically plied the Judge with a shot of bourbon he'd refuse on aesthetic, not legal, grounds, and sister Sissie was rubbing her snatch against the knee of an Arab, Vince Mansur, who ignored her, looking off to the side at three nervously underage college girls who looked like they were trying to look like triplets, swarthy Vince no doubt figuring they'd be worth it if he could get them all at once; and they played at ignoring him, giggling and experimenting with derision, seeking in the trapped smoke of tavern extrafirma a rarefication of bitchery that would prevent them from evaporating under the overt intentions of Vince's stare through the haze, between the torsos milling with the inscrutability of insidious purpose, that is not to say *incidus porpoise* as one is tempted at the sudden sail in of sailors, three swablings hauling their easy malice into the terra incognito under the whip, lash and hooves of Frankie's "Mule Train," to immediately begin disparaging the one singer who ever made the Wurlitzer worth my nickel. Would that I were ignorant of their trifling taunts! But I was sitting too close to the door.

I stood and hovered about the tarry trio in a state of dismay, regretting the untimely end of the Korean conflict, examining their sparsely pelted heads for warts, crannies, lobal irregularities, concavities, incipient tumors, any phrenological explanation for their aversion to Frankie Laine. I went so far as to follow as they made their way to the bar casting obscenities Laineward, as they purchased three bottles of the local elixir, their voices loud and alien, shipwrecked, shoreleft, the nickel change helixing to rest on the bar an independent arrogance—Ernest, the bartender, didn't look at it, pick it up—and I continued to follow them as they headed back as straight as the tables and the gamboling revelers would allow to the jukebox, wondering now why if their short pants served any purpose they weren't even shorter and further trying to distinguish in their deck scampering gaits a unity of acquiescence, a benign potential to their landing here at the Iwo Jima of my night life. Alas and fuck me heinie, no luck to be had!

Do not forsake me oh my darlin, Frankie began, and I knew what was going to happen, before Frankie could get another word out, that the one of the three built like me, tall and thin, though being a sailor likely endowed with *ropelike* arms—the other two adhered to type, one short and simian like a thyroid dwarf, the other red of hair and face, pimply too, and larger than he himself, dim certainly of wit, could ever entirely comprehend—I knew he would forsake Frankie and he did, muttering some watery curse and slamming his hip into the

Wurlitzer, the needle slashing the disc like a feline fingernail opening a wound on a back, Frankie letting out the cut shriek of a garroted mink, the ensuing silence slung low as an aurora borealis across the firm terra of the tavern.

The offending sailor, in elaborate pretense of heedlessness, spread his wingspan over the machine as if looking to select a song or two himself, one of which was already tattooing its banality into his skull, for he tapped his Old Style against the side of the Wurlitzer as he looked down at the reflection of his smirk.

Hey Sailor! wouldn't do, nor the old Avast, Cutpurse!, so I silently approached arear his left flank under the thuggish scrutiny of his cronies, who appraised me for threat and found me wanting. Yet I wasn't, the thing was thrust upon me. I am weak and a pleasant drunk. Yet Frankie forsuck: forsooth, I must needs act.

I leaned on the Wurlitzer and looked my enemy in the eyes. They weren't more than a foot from mine.

"Take a hike, pissant," he said, and immediately a little mahatma appeared in my mind and warned, "Watch the dwarf."

"Frank Miller?" I said, a little more Palance than Cooper.

One pool ball knocked another to let me know that the bar was anxious to resume its farrago.

"No, you got the wrong guy so get lost."

"These your boys, Frank?" I asked, indicating the seagoyles on either side of him, at the same time taking in the crowd to measure it for likelihood of intervention. I thought I could be reasonably sure they'd prevent my being beaten to death.

"I'm not Frank," the sailor said.

I waited for him to guzzle his beer. His pals were radiating the stupid rapture of anticipated violence.

"I know'd you'd come, Frank."

With an unnerving aplomb he shifted the bottle to get agrip its neck. That meant he probably wasn't carrying a knife.

"I said I'm not Frank," he said, carefully exploring the contours of his implicit threat by narrowing his eyes.

Why am I doing this?, I asked myself as I watched the baby mahatma take flight down a bright street, rapidly losing ground to a small white barking dog.

"Oh, you're Frank all right, and here to make trouble."

He turned to furrow his brows at the homunculus—a hair too tall to deliver any luck—hoping the homunculus and I would understand without a word, at precisely the same time, that though he didn't know what to make of me he was still going to have to beat me up.

I couldn't shut up.

"I'm afraid," I said, "I'm going to have to ask you to hand over that bottle."

What made that the last straw I couldn't say, but his left shot out in an open face jab, slapping low, into my chest and bouncing me off the paneling. His right had the bottle cocked over his ear, sizing me up for one good swipe, and in the instant before I reacted to save my scalp I noticed his crew had turned for crowd control, leaving me alone for the nonce with aforesaid weapon.

"Wait—the Wurlitzer!" I shouted, pointing up at a far corner of the zincplate ceiling, and when he looked up that way I administered a hard, awkward, left-hand backhand to his neck, a sort of rebound shot that used some of the force I brought with me off the wall, yet lacked smoothness for the hesitation inherent in the smack as an alternative to using the bottle I held in my right and natural hand. The force of the blow, coupled with the surprise and no doubt sickly feeling that he'd been had, and easily, rendered the swabbie useless long enough for me to dart past him and squeeze tween his minions toward the crowd that didn't yet know if it could resume dancing and mingling or still had to wait for a bottle to lay open a brow, and thus served monolithically a moment to thwart me. I paused and turned and there was that same goddamned empty Old Style bottle approaching my head, for he had spun, oh wise watery warthead, and *then* swung fore and down at my head whereat my panic forthwithwhich I was able to adjust my sense of time, slowing it down, slowing the bottle down, giving myself just enough time to duck and sidesquirm tween Sissie and some slaggard, so that the arm hanging from the bottle fell against my shoulder, whereupon someone shouted in the time that sped up to account for the lag, "What?" and someone else shouted, "He hit Sissie with a bottle!" and I was jostled by the pandemonium from the less adventitious fix of being between the crowd and my assailant to the other side of a quarantine that kept the dwarf and the rogue Irish thug baby from coming to the aid of their pummeled pal, who had just split open the skullskin of the gal with the most brothers available in the bar, and before long I had my back against said bar, Judge Swiggum at my elbow, a cold beer in my hand, and I was watching two sailors astride and heaving a fluked flunkey brush past Joe Turner at the door, too grateful over their own escape to congratulate Joe on his bloody knuckles.

Todd Mills

As the political reporter I took the occasional interest in politics. Nothing much of interest happened any more, but I had a good memory. When Kennedy was shot I was in high school in Milwaukee.

"When Evelyn disappeared, Eisenhower was president."

"Was he?"

"And Nixon was vice-president."

"I suppose that's true. I was just in high school so I never took an interest. Not to imply I did later take an interest. But Bobby knew all that stuff."

How does one begin to ask why Larry was locked in the cellar? Adele and I were adrift. When you've been in the same place a long time, it's pleasant to drift.

"How old was he? In 1953."

"20s. Maybe late 20s."

The specificity of her answer, the meanings it could imply, opened a chasm between us as wide as her history.

"Do you know who he voted for?"

"I don't even know who was running, but not Eisenhower, that's for sure. He and his friend Steve hated Eisenhower. I remember one time he told me, Stella, people who work in gas stations don't vote Republican. One of his few political lessons. The night Evelyn was killed he had sent me home to put lipstick on and do my hair up like a lady. That was a political lesson, too. Make it easier for people to break the rules for us, he said. So I calculated that I was at my house when Evelyn was killed, at my lower middle class house like a good girl. Safe at home. Unlike the upper middle class girl who was unsafe at someone else's upper middle class home. Of course, I didn't stay home long."

Bobby, Oct. 24, 1953

Sitting next to Judge Hamilton Swiggum was to know what it was like to be the peak nearest Everest, shoulder to shoulder and miles away. You didn't turn to Judge Swiggum and ask casually,

"How's everything, Judge?" If he wanted you to know, he'd tell you, and then you'd think you were Moses. Yet my successful escape from harm's way had livened up my spirit and I felt no height was too steep, or something equally inexpressible having to do with the human spirit admixed with alcohol. I turned to the Judge and watched his face a while, wondering what it would take to establish myself as a recognizable inhabitant of his planet. Not that I wanted to sport with him; no one never did that. Maybe I just found myself in a democratic mood. The Judge sat perfectly erect, his spine drilled at 90 degrees into his bar stool, staring straight ahead at the terraced bottles behind the bar. His head was gigantic (Homeric!), capped by a veritable wavy sea (Homeric!) of silver. Wild white tufts were planted eccentrically above his eyes and in his ears. I studied the man with such care, between surveys of the bar to see if Stella had arrived, that I became anxious with admiration for his method of delivering drink to mouth, an operation as rigid and triangular as the manipulations of a boom crane. While there's nothing romantic about a boom crane, the Judge's absorption in a ritual of his own devising struck me as saturate with romance, the romance expected of us by the gods. I was getting mighty thirsty.

Eventually these rituals brought about the need for a sort of mother ritual.

"**Ernest**," the Judge boomed, so that if Ernest were tending bar across the street instead of several feet down he would still have heard, "**the same**."

Ernest immediately abandoned the drink he was laboring over, plucked a fresh glass from under the bar, and removed a bottle of vodka from the Judge's line of sight. Under the Judge's enormous left hand, veined like a steep mountain, lay a pile of neatly stacked ones.

"The czar is dead," I said, "yet his life's blood lives still. Isn't that the way of it, Judge?"

If I haven't gotten it across, what's most remarkable about the Judge is his power to exclude anyone he likes from the courtroom he moves around in. Or so it seems. At the Coo Coo Club in the Judge's world, there was a bar at which he sat, a familiar man who tended it, and a short obstacle course to the bathroom. I was a mystifying intrusion. He swiveled his head my way with his geometric precision, precisely 90 degrees, and lowered it 15 degrees to look me in the eyes.

"**Are you being philosophical with me, boy?**"

"I am," I said, with no little courage.

"**Why?**"

"Well, sir, I suppose I'm cadging for a beer."

He swiveled his skull another 45 degrees to examine the bottle in my hand, which was about half-full.

"**Son**," he said, "**you have a bottle of beer in your hand**."

"That's true, sir," I replied. "I'd like to have one in my other hand."

I could see by the subtle contraction of his incongruously youthful lips that I had successfully appealed to the free-floating habit of his jurisprudence. I imagined hopefully that he saw me as a blindfolded lady, off-balance by one beer.

And as if he had run our negotiations through in their whimsical entirety, he finally said, "**There remains the issue of money.**"

"You don't think they charge too much..."

"**Quite the contrary, lad. The issue concerns the provider of the money.**"

"The provider of the money."

"**He who pays.**"

Ernest established his complicity in my impromptu scheme by holding the Judge's drink just out of his reach for the duration of our deliberations, probably the decisive factor, for in effect, in de facto fashion, he was appending my transaction with the Judge to the Judge's with his, and as the Judge cared not to exist long between drinks, he was inclined to favor a quick resolution; yet addicted to his private juridical standards—let there be no doubt—he found it necessary to rifle his files of memory for precedent, an afflicted and uncertain process that could find me impatient to drink. After all, there must be moments of sobriety in even this Judge's life, and they would be filled with the pleasures of puzzling out law.

"I merely thought, Judge Swiggum," I rushed headlong, "that it would be far easier for you to pay as your money is literally right here at hand while mine is presently squirming in a dwindling bank account. At the moment I am broke."

"**Ernest**," Swiggum gaveled, "**a drink for the boy**," and as Ernest complied I could see that the decision had not relieved the entirety of pressure the conundrum inflicted on the Judge about the swirling gray temples. Silent lammergeiers diminished between us, wafted high by invisible currents of frosty air.

"**Ernest**," he added, "**be sure to replace the boy's bottles as he places them empty upon the bartop**."

"Thanks, Judge," I said, but he was already back in his chambers.

As a sort of misguided tribute to me and my defense of what's right in music, some patron or other had released the inferior inflections of Tex Ritter's "High Noon" into the atmosphere. Nick Turner was beginning to turn things around on the pool table, his brother Joe leaning against the cue rack as if he hadn't just bare-knuckled unconscious a belligerent navvy, now gauging the temperament of the two college boys who were about to lose the rest of their lunch money for the term; the Eau Claire salesman spent the few dollars he'd been allowed to win befriending Mitzie Skumsrud, a wealthy poker widow down the bar where at least once a week she found herself a symmetrix to the Judge, matching him in hard liquor drop for drop, though they didn't drink it that way; Vince had his hirsute, intransigently mammal arm on the back of the chair of one of the three college girls, who shifted constantly, her virginity something small and trapped in her eyes. Her friends closed in on Vince gradually, conversing with unnatural animation, gesticulating like his ancestors in a coffee shop planning the assassination by knife of some flunky Turk.

Sissie held a towel of ice cubes to her head and looked like she was feeling mean. As fewer than five years had passed since we had fucked, she drifted up to the bar to take it out on me.

"Where's your little teenage tart?"

"Have a beer," I said, thrusting an Old Style toward the cleavage she habitually offered for refuge.

"Thanks," she said. "So where is the little slut?"

"Let me see the wound—you might need stitches."

"No, it's barely cut. But there's a lump like an egg already."

She pulled the towel away and showed me. Sure enough, the towel was just a little pink, and an egg was rising into her hairline.

"It was real brave the way you picked a fight and let me take the blow."

"Can't you be nice, Sis?"

"Not to a guy who manhandles children and runs from other men."

"Look, Sis, you can't have it both ways. Either she's a child or she's a slut…or tart. She can't be both, or all three, or if she is she's entitled to our respect, not to mention gives me license."

"Either way it's illegal. How old is she?"

"22."

"Like hell. I happen to know she's a sophomore in high school. She's 16 tops."

Suddenly I realized this was a bad conversation to have next to a judge. You could just hear the Judge declaiming, "**The law is never off duty, son. Hand over the girl**."

I swung around to the bar, my knees working with Sissie's like interlocking gears to bring her along with me. I hung my arm on her shoulders, brought my face near to the flesh rising bulbous from her dress, and lowered my voice, conspirator-like.

"Sis," I confided, "don't tell *anyone* this, not a soul. Promise?"

She promised with the specific alacrity of one eager to betray a trust.

"The fact is—and you promised to tell no one—the fact is, Sis, I've been forced to be honorable by a medical condition. I'm impotent, Sis. The little dip is just for show, see, and her hymen, praise be to God, is intact."

Sissie's laughter seemed to begin inside, and bubble up out of, her oft-manhandled breasts.

"You're such an asshole," she laughed out, "such a lying, stinking asshole." She had me pegged, of course, but here's where her nymphomania kicks in. While she knows I'm lying to get her off my back, the very topic lubricates her and she can no longer decipher the context of the situation.

Her hand slapped down on my knee and slid up my thigh, and she purred predictably, "I think I can help you with that problem," and had it really been a problem so simple was it to solve, but next thing I feel is above my waist—that is, a pain screaming from my arm where Stella had it and was giving it the Romanian burn.

"Christ!" I prayed, and she dropped my arm to turn on Sissie.

"A few minutes late and you have to start in on this of all sluts?" she upbraided me, looking with heartrending challenge straight into Sissie's eyes.

And judging by the sudden wash of glee over Sissie's face, the catfight would've been on had Buzzy not thereupon stiff-armed the tavern door and Grouchoed across the floor at too high a speed directly toward the three of us, all betwixt stepping timely aside as if in choreograph, one sleeve of Buzzy's jacket swaying in front of him like an elephant's trunk, a sizeable triangle of his shirt slouching through the open zipper of his pants, a genuinely stricken look on his face, coming on so fast I yanked Stella out of his way, removing the only cushion between Buzzy and the solid mahogany of the bar itself, which he caromed off sideways into Sissie, one of whose breasts Buzzy could not help helping himself to on his way down, leaving the one-armed feller with nothing to grab the bar.

Sporting Stella, a good egg all round, forgot her quarrel and helped Sissie help Buzzy up, nearly sliding his jacket off trying to pull him up by the empty sleeve. Sissie knew where the extant arm was, and so was of more help, yet it was together they got Buzzy back up and on balance and faced him to the bar. I helped by stifling my laughter so I could hear him tell whatever phantom his possessed eyes glimpsed in the vacancy between himself and his next drink, "Something happened... something bad happened," repeating it over and over until Ernest got between him and his ghost and handed over a shot of whiskey, on the house.

Buzzy tossed the potion back toward his punching bag, tucked his chin into the shoulder that had an arm hanging from it, and made a sound like a muzzled horse sneezing. His eyes focused on me, and the smile of Preacher Casey spread on his face like an Okie dawn.

"Almost got caught," he said. "Something broke up the poker game, and Hopkins came right home. Had to go out the window. Jesus: out the window like a goddamn burglar—good thing they didn't have the storms up yet..."

Marla Rothgert

The days scroll by. The days scroll by like camels in the desert...

Chorus

See her, see her through the plate-glass window, sitting
in her red side-zippered pants, legs curled up under
the innocence of her maturing hip, reading a book,
her glasses aslant, one foot in its bobby sock cocoon
tapping to music you can faintly hear on this side of
the glass, where it's dark, and you are oblivious of the
threat intrinsic to this composition, the shades open,
the young girl, the dark leering stranger, the shape of
the bra through the white cotton blouse, the absorption of a 15-year-old girl, the muted tin of the radio
music, a situation cornered by itself, a circle complet-
ing itself, a conspiracy, time turning back on itself so
that an adamantine horror, autonomous, latent, regal,
can imagine for us no other scenario than the noise
heard in the basement, faint as the tin of the music
on this side of the glass, the tilt of the girl's head, at
first vaguely curious, that's all, a little noise, a little
tilt of the head, like a kitty cat coming briefly out of
a dream, the latent horror now splitting her sense of
time as it splits yours, like a plate-glass window you
see her through, one Evelyn who believes not in the
noise in the basement, and the other Evelyn who has
already seen the shape of the terror, the hair on its

arms, the implacability of its intent like a hurricane inside the tiny noise, the darkness of its reason, see her face in rictal increments express her acquiescence to the madness of this scene, and her other face looking back into her book at words that refuse to move and she listens to music already becoming a detail, already estranged, an aspect required for our credulity, the way our own paralysis and penumbral vision lends acuity to Evelyn's senses so that she can hear a foot slide across the basement's cement floor and feel in the very stillness following that same shape of what was no longer moving, coming straight for her, see her, look at the baby and look at the wolf, her uncivilized grasp of danger distorted by a cultivated disbelief that fails to destroy the hope riveting her to her chair as the wolf charges up the stairs in its death rush, springing, its back arched and massive, Evelyn unversed in panic simulating a scream no louder than the radio, knocked off the table, still playing in the absence of carnage that holds you in its sway like a painting that subtly reduces the distortions of the real, the radio with its tail disappearing into the wall, Evelyn's glasses upside-down a few feet away unable to rid themselves of their palpable meaning, unable to stop looking or look away, and in our beds looking at the ceiling at night for the last thing seen through the lenses...

Todd Mills

What rankles—yes, I still use the word rankles—is the interment of the event. Long after Evelyn was taken, another woman, Terry Dollowy, was killed. And I have trouble remembering whether it was her headless body found burning beside a highway south of town, or her bodiless head in a heap of ashes.

"Yesterday," I told Adele, "a reporter spent the day up there, by Winona. And there's a bar nearby, in Pickwick, a small town, and he said it became a sort of Evelyn central, where reporters gathered to wait for the bulldozers to finish their job. It may sound pretentious to you, but when I got the assignment to go up there today—of course, yesterday they were unable to complete the work—I had no interest in involving myself in the camaraderie of this..."

"It's a spectacle now," she said.

"But it wasn't then, was it? And despite my emotional detachment from the case—after all, when it happened I was 4 years old, living in Milwaukee—despite that, I had no stomach for a kind of camaraderie of..."

"Vultures."

"No, it's not that bad..."

And there was a woman whose name I can never recall, killed in her home up a dead-end road off Mormon Coulee Road, way on the south end of town. At the time Evelyn was killed this area would have been out of town. Evelyn could well have been ditched there, or near there, or buried there. They had found what may have been Evelyn's undergarments under the overpass nearby. They think the killer drove a truck or a van, and the whole thing was terribly bloody. Maybe the victim was wrapped in the shower curtain, maybe it was a bedspread. But the case is forgotten, more or less. The name and face are gone. It's Evelyn's name that's here, and that photo of her in glasses that is printed in every anniversary recapitulation. Evelyn arises a genius loci of murdered women who return to Evelyn, to a photograph, a triumph for eternal murder.

And in some mid-region looms the sadistic Adele Markham…

There were no photographs of herself on the wall, only rather common still lives of flowers.

I recalled that an outside investigator was brought in to solve the case, a modern criminologist with a lie detector. Hundreds of high school and college students were tested before an outcry put a stop to the practice.

"Did you take the lie detector test?" I asked Adele.

"Only the boys were given the test."

It was as if the world was small enough, as if the murder took place in an Agatha Christie drawing room.

And then came the raw realization of a yawning infinite.

"Do you remember if they stopped giving the test because of a public outcry, or was there some other reason?"

"I remember that Bobby and One-Arm Buzzy thought the idea was hilarious. Everything to do with the investigator—Schmidt, Investigator Schmidt. He was a continual source of laughs for those two."

One-Arm Buzzy

I liked to drive the side streets to Maggie's house. I would zigzag until the last possible moment to prolong the suspense. She worked it out like this: there was a streetlight that lit up a semi-circle in front of her house where her old man Johnnie parked his car. The other side of the street was dark. When Johnnie went to work the night shift, the first car that took his place was the one that got Maggie. You had to time it right because Maggie figured if every time Johnnie left he'd see a car down the street start up he'd figure out what was going on, which was probably true.

So when I turned on the street before, Farnam Avenue, if there was a car on the street it was Bobby making out with Stella. They parked in the shade. Across from them was a driveway for some of the houses and an alley behind where the houses had garages. Those garages are why nobody ever needed to park on the dark side of the street across from Maggie and Bobby's place.

Bobby and Stella had a bet going on about who would get to Maggie first. The bet was just for fun, which rankled me because why make a bet if you're not going to pay. They would name a figure, say five bucks, and Bobby won every time but never collected. Stella never paid. I understand she might not have the money, but then they should make some other arrangement so that figure isn't always there. I could think of ways she could pay.

The steering on my truck could be a problem, so when I would make the corner and wave at them the truck would be half up the curve and I'd just miss the tree, a big elm tree on the side of the road like it was placed there just to be an obstacle for me. There wasn't one across the street, which would make it easier to park there, but then I wouldn't get Maggie as a reward. And no matter how cold it was, Bobby and Stella would be parked there with the engine off and their hands inside each other's clothes.

Bobby, Spring, 1954

Not a minute before Buzzy came by my mind zimmed off toward a second plane without for a moment abandoning the erminical trollop beside me, my Stella, whom I suddenly looked back on from the year two thousand as a dim, dimming, or gone memory while every stretch of Evelyn's contour from my two brief sightings of her remained stark, vivid, and clean.

"All right," I was telling Stella, who was again stuck on the question of why if I could dip into her teens I could not conceive of her dipping *out* of them, that is to take her seriously, "all right, my little otter, maybe we will never break up, you and I, our love is mad, delirious, and final"—here she made a face and kicked me, as if I needed a reminder that she had yet to turn 16 the nickel change helixing to rest on the bar an independent arrogance. We had made our points, but the points my mind was making were nippled nothings, accessories to optional future emotional breakthroughs. There we were, huddled against the cold of a false spring March night, on Maggie surveillance, my hand trapped inside Stella's bra and so impaled by her sharp little nipple, and I could not elude the thought of that Evenipple, briefly seen, never feared, that last fall, half a year before, maybe less than two months before she was killed.

I didn't know Evelyn, of course—I met Stella because she ranged into my territory, not because I ranged into hers. I was filling my lighter at the fluid dispenser at Zimmers, my mind on nothing more extruse than the predominance of nickels in my pocket, not a single penny, half attent to the door because Stella was due in sooner or later—my mind I should say was positively lolling in the luxury of its own calm, its sargasso of banalities: how I loved waiting for a woman I knew would arrive! When in from a churlish afternoon chill charged a womanchild with breasts hidden behind three chaste layers of white, though a nipple not much smaller than a thumb pressed through on the right, which is why I bring it and them up. A folded piece of paper was in the pocket on the other side, leaving but that one super-raisin that so rapidly reneged like some timid vermifauna. With a woman's self-possession she snapped a nickel on the counter, grabbed a paper, and took a step toward the door; and with a girl's absorption suddenly she turned—as if to emblazon an image in the mind of a stranger—looked my way, and turned again to leave, just a nice high school girl with an autonomous evanescence of nipple picking up a newspaper for daddy while mommy shopped next door. Turns out that was Evelyn Hartley.

Hopkins had emerged on schedule at 10:15, loping carward with his steel lunch bucket, down the walk, around the back of his car, into the mischievous stagelight aimed at his cuckoldry that made this nightly spectacle seem all the more a distillation of an amazing organized cruelty.

"Look at that poor bastard," I said. He even had orange hair and a ruddy simpleton's face.

He paused with his hand on the door handle before climbing into his car, and it was difficult not to imagine he was contemplating the contentment provided by his complete delusion.

"He always seems so happy," Stella said.

"Sure, he's in a great mood—and Buzzy's going to be drilling his wife in a few minutes."

"Nope," Stella insisted, "the Fruit from Beirut."

"I don't know why you insist on betting. I told you Buzzy only goes out of his way to tell me his plans for the night when he really plans on mounting the lady Hopkins. It never fails."

"The Fruit from Beirut was here the last two Wednesdays."

By now Hopkins was in his car. The dome light was on, but I couldn't see Hopkins.

"Well, maybe he *is* coming, but Buzzy will win the race."

Hopkins popped back upright.

"Ah, there he is…"

"I hope he never finds out," Stella said as Hopkins drove past us with dome light on so we could get a good look at what it's like to be duped five or six times a week. "He's not such a poor bastard if he never finds out."

"Right, if your wife's getting fucked and you're not around, does she moan…I get nervous when broads talk that way."

"I'd never cheat *you*, hon," she said, and that was when she captured my hand in the trap of her bra, a gesture accomplished with virtuoso alacrity, and the nipples in my mind were like the stars of a summer night…

But the world gorges itself on complexities and then belches out static across the sublime. Buzzy came too fast around the corner as always, waved at us, lost control of his truck, and barely avoided the tree in front of Maggie's, and his truck only returned entirely to the pavement when it reached the circle of light that awaited him.

One-Arm Buzzy

I always liked to tell Bobby I had a poker game going or something, maybe I was going to a movie, because the first time I went to Maggie I was a little embarrassed and I lied and now that's what he expected me to do and somehow I couldn't break out of it. What are you doing tonight, Buzz? And I said, thinking rapidly, going to a movie, and by 10 the next morning three people have told Bobby, Guess whose truck I saw in front of the Hopkins place? Which was fine by me, since I told Bobby everything anyway. I guess it's a habit to fulfill expectations, or maybe that's how habits get started.

Maggie was more than a habit to me, though I always felt a little uncomfortable that I was nothing more than part of a habit to her. I loved her. How else to explain going back after the night I almost got caught, the night Evelyn Hartley was killed, as if I didn't have enough to remember it by. Jesus H. Christ, the phone rang and she said, "What? He can't do this to me!" And I knew what happened, that he was already on his way home, and goddamnit from the minute I stepped into that house the first time it bothered me that there was a door in front and the other on the side. I don't like a house with a front door and no back door. The only way to go out the back was through the bedroom window, and I *had* to go out the back because the Brewhouse where they held the game was but five minutes' drive from there. He could be in the driveway for all I knew.

Later on I recounted the whole thing to Bobby and he was particularly interested in what Maggie said, "He can't do this to me!," which he thought was pretty flattering, and I guess it was pretty flattering, but up to that time I was a little too caught up in the momentum of flight to give a rat's pecker for the particulars.

I guess one of the detectives was in on the game.

Todd Mills

I tried to imagine what Adele looked like back then. The gulf between now and then sickened me.

I could not imagine a 15-year-old Adele Markham, or a racy Stella with her 30-year-old boyfriend.

Yet that she was once forty years younger and knew none of the coming forty years seemed to me an intolerable torment.

"What happened to Bobby?"

"What do you mean?"

Her face assumed an expression stricken with an almost squeamish surprise.

"Never mind."

"Will you have some coffee now, Dick?"

I would, I nodded. She rose noiselessly, with the economy of a woman in an old television ad.

I realized that I had been making a face, as if I had been eating bad tripe.

I wonder if there is good tripe.

"Buzzy owned a gas station," she said over her shoulder. And when she returned she said, "Buzzy owned the gas station where Bobby worked. When I returned to the Coo Coo Club, just after I got there Buzzy came in shaken up because he had almost been caught in bed with another man's wife."

"That same night? That Evelyn was killed?"

"Good thing he never had to give his alibi."

The coffee was instant, and it was too strong. Evelyn, I thought, would have asked if I wanted cream or sugar.

"You don't have to drink it."

First the tripe, then the coffee.

The whole scenario.

Larry in the cellar.

I looked at my watch then up at Adele, observing me with an admixture of sarcasm and appeal. Spasms of distant panic broke towards me, expiring between my chair and the door.

"I can't picture you back then," I blurted.

"Back then," she said, shifting her weight.

"Yes."

"Back then I was a happy little truant, 30 pounds lighter, with a sharp tongue, perky breasts, not a thought about the future, madly in love...people said I looked like Natalie Wood when I was in my early 20s."

"Did Evelyn's death have an effect on you—I mean a lasting effect?"

"Is that what's troubling you? I thought it was just locking my husband in the cellar—"

"It's that, too."

She waited until she was sure I was alert to her reaction before she laughed, a short, mean laugh.

"I don't really think it's possible to say. When I think of that night the first thing I think of is Buzzy almost getting caught because of Evelyn's murder, and how we had no idea the two were connected."

"As if Evelyn's abduction were a sort of background noise you recalled later."

"Right. Her *abduction*." This, clearly, *was* mockery. "Like a stray clam."

"What do you mean?"

"I don't think so."

"Don't think so what?"

"I don't think Evelyn's death was any different from any other event that stands out in a person's youth. A lot of things happen and you live through them. Or maybe I just don't want my own recent fiasco to be considered something that changes anybody's lives."

"No offense."

"None possible."

Like a stray clam, she had said.

Bobby, Oct. 24, 1953

Liquor, I've often noticed, lubricates centripetally, and it's a beautiful thing to observe, when aggression sops away into sloppy sentimental sippery, bitcheries calm into wary regard to make way for that gregarious suppressed ghost, the inner gossip, to emerge and mingle avidly with all the disparates about. Buzzy explained the card game, nodding downbar to Mitzie Skumsrud (once, of course, Skumsruud), and perhaps it was the inevitable prognisticatory comparison or some other attraction contained in the *Homo Katatastrophus*—the two girlchilds likely even sensing the similarities they already shared—but I watched them come together like natural conspirators, Stella's jealousy anyway a fickle trait, a form of camouflage, and Sissie too nympho to care much about the allure of another—already she looked like she'd settled on Buzzy for the night, which is not necessarily to say that sometimes a good knock on the head can go either way.

Buzzy was explaining about the game, but I was stuck on the mechanics of the escape, that "out the window like a goddamn burglar."

"Usually you think of a burglar going *in* a window—I mean in terms of imagery—"

"Shut up, asshole," Sissie said.

"Not if the husband's coming home you don't."

"Look," Stella said, "you can tell him to shut up, but you can't call him an asshole."

Sissie just smiled and said, "Go on, Buzzy, tell her about the poker game."

Mitzie Skumsrud had her elbows propped on the bar, fingers steepled together, thumbs holding her drink in place, remarkable skinny torso leaning forward, all so that she could accomplish the getting of soused with the absolute maximum of economy—the swinging of fingers and thumbs working in high concert/low exertion to approximate with the glass the motion of a birdswing, swinging higher and higher, the liquid level getting lower and lower.

"She looks like a grasshopper," Stella said somewhere in the midst of it all, and Sissie laughed the loudest, and one of the two referred to Mitzie as an old bag, and that was when Buzzy put his narrational foot down.

"Well that old bag," Buzzy said, "is married to the richest man in La Crosse."

"And bored as she is," I added, "She'll shanghai that boring bunghole beside her before the night is through."

"Because she hates her husband, who runs a poker game at the Brewhouse bar, a private game, a couple of the brewery execs—"

"And various other scheming elites—"

"One of which—"

"Whom."

"Shut up."

"Asshole."

"Ladies… One of which is John Hopkins' uncle, who is welcome at the table because he's a moron, but not so much a moron he can't see that nephew John is a darn good card player—"

"Who's his uncle?" Sissie asked.

Buzzy, who after all had had the only hand he had on one of Sissie's breasts, resituated himself as if her interest were an invitation—I say as if it weren't—swiveling to lean against the bar, running his arm along behind the bar to draw Sissie in closer to the tangible significance of his words.

"Hekler," Buzzy said. "The realtor. The one who burned up those farms and bought up the land. Hopkins' mother's sister married Hekler's brother, the one with the skin disease, the one who dyes his chest hair."

"Another whiskey, Buzz?" I offered, remembering again the proximity of a judge to our huddle. He could have heard every word, but his remoteness of bearing assimilated him in with the rest of the bar props. Mitzie, on the other hand, though close enough I could've hit her with a spit ice cube, could be assumed to be far enough gone in several enough ways she couldn't have heard us even without the music, some new form of torture I suspected one of Vince's college girls of purchasing. There was a physicality to her besotten conversation with the man beside her as of two overlubricated machine parts sloshing off one another.

"I've seen that guy," Stella cringed, "He's like a walking disease. I've seen him at the pool hall on the north side."

The pool hall on the north side. A better man would have taken her aside and given her the third degree. But a better man would have spanked her for everything we did together.

"Ernest, another for Buzzy when you get a chance."

"…something broke up the game, I don't know what, but the runner, that Markham boy, Stella's cousin, right?, he had the good sense to call Maggie's, which give me just enough time to get my clothes on and that's it before I heard the front door and dodged out the winder like a, you listening Bobby?, like a goddamned *burglar*."

And with a fluency that can't be taught he turned to grab his whiskey just as Ernest was setting it down, gulped its entirety without melodrama, and exclaimed with evident exhilaration, "Jesus, that makes a guy feel like his arm could grow back."

And it may seem odd, overly mystical, but at that moment it seemed to me that slovenly sleeve on Stella's side of my best friend and boss was empty so we could fill it up with our happiness, the four of us, cuddling serendipetally in the space we left open for just this or something like this, the Coo Coo Club at eve and ease, never more than now a real environment, a veritable liquor storm of consciousnesses ranging from benevolent to indifferent, no hostiles, the hour still early enough that all impending emotional disasters were still forestallable by simulacrae of hope; archetypes were still archetypes and it would be hours before the booze would break them down into the specificities of variegated humanity; the virgins could still rest on hymens as pristine as brand new leather bicycle seats; a salesman could count up his change and catch a cab and Mitzie could let him go without embarrassing herself; and one of the pool-playing college boys could still put on some hillbilly music and the mood of the whole tavern could lift yet another notch, unregrettable hours sailing past...

Todd Mills

I noticed there was no television in the room, and for that matter no books. What does one do when one's husband is locked in the cellar?

There were no magazines in a wicker basket.

Perhaps her bedroom was another universe, of pills, dank sheets, wine, bad faith, insomnia.

Bad nerves, anyway, I knew something about.

An abrupt brightness occurred, very much an event from beyond the windows in the room, the sun finally broken free of clouds, dimmed only by the white shades, a modest jolt of surprise around a corner.

Adele was laughing, or trying to get herself to laugh. There always seemed two aspects of personality working in her at one time.

"Did you know about the campaign to clear all the cars in the city?"

"Clear them?"

"Of guilt. There was a drive, so to speak, to get everyone to take their cars, voluntarily, to the gas stations, where they would be checked by attendants, like Bobby. If there were no bodies in the back seat or in the trunk they would get a little sticker put on their car that said, 'My Car is OK.'"

"That is funny," I said. "No I didn't know about that."

"Of course, this was before Inspector Schmidt came. This was maybe two or three days after the crime. You want a big change to come out of the crime, here it is. You want to know what *effect* the crime had? The first day of the sticker campaign Bobby invented the self-service gas station. There were so many cars lined up he couldn't do everything, so he had people fill their own tanks while he checked the trunks and the back seats..."

"So people took it seriously? As if the killer would be the only person in La Crosse whose car had no sticker?"

By now Adele had again lost the bitter edge that seemed to expand and contract in her like a quality of moonlight.

"Or as if the killer would show up with blood all over the back seat and that's how they'd catch him. It was remarkable how many people showed up, too, how quickly word got around. Do you believe in collective guilt?"

"I don't really understand the idea."

"Well, it seems to me everybody was feeling pretty guilty the way they rushed to clear themselves."

"It seems more of a collective hand-wringing, of guilt."

"The opposite of guilt. I think that's how Bobby saw it. He didn't have a car, but he put a sticker on Buzzy's truck. He played along for the fun of it. Suddenly a lowly gas station attendant had the power to declare people innocent or guilty."

"How long did this go on?"

"A few days. I don't remember. A year later you'd still see them. And they were hard to get off, too…"

"Was there any protest? Wouldn't the implication be that any car without a sticker would be stopped and searched?"

She looked at me with a sort of patient bemusement, as if I had just sat in on a conversation she was having with someone else.

I thought she could possibly be insane.

"I really have no idea, Todd."

Peter Kurten, the Dusseldorf Murderer

In July 1913 I went up to the first floor of the house on the corner of the Munster and Ulmenstrasse. I had a chopper with me. I had been to the house once already to steal. I was just about to cleave through the head of the 16-year-old girl when a man jumped out of bed. I ran away, throwing the chopper on the bed as I ran.

Marla Rothgert

Al Patros…Al Patros…Al Batros…Albatross…Albatross! Albatross! Albatross!

Bobby, Oct. 28, 1953

"You think Evelyn Hartley is in my trunk?" the guy asked.

I recognized him. He sold cars.

"By that logic, I'd have to say *you* think Evelyn Hartley is in your trunk. You pulled up here. I didn't invite you. And of course you're free to change your mind."

The poor bastard's life was a common and natural bifurcation: obsequious on the job, arrogant off the job, the two halves joined by the inability to keep his mouth shut. At work he was cloying charm manifest, elsewhere a shitstorm of misappropriated cleverness and transparent postures. Worse, he had longlobed ears that swung like doors to 90 degrees relative his face.

He idled his fresh-off-the-lot Buick at Buzzy's Skelly, where he came to let me know that he didn't much like the idea of a peon like myself checking his trunk for the corpse of a 15-year-old girl.

"Just give me one of those stickers," he said impatiently, betraying the weakness of his position.

I kept the stickers in my left hand where he couldn't stop glancing at them. I had the impression he was the whole time on the brink of making a grab for them.

"Gladly," I said, with cloying charm, "just as soon as I check your trunk."

"I'm not letting some gas station flunky in my trunk. You're not the law, pal."

"Okay," I said, turning to walk back inside.

"Wait. Get back here. I'm not leaving until I get a sticker."

I strolled back to his car and leaned down close to his face.

"Mister," I said, though he was about my age, "the sticker says, 'My Car is OK,' and until I check your trunk, your car is not OK."

I craned my neck to get a good look at his back seat.

"For that matter, I'm not even sure your back seat is OK. What's that stain?"

He looked over his shoulder, letting out a little burp of panic.

"What stain?"

"Right there, right behind you."

He screwed around further to look.

"Where?"

"Right there on the seat. How long has that stain been there?"

"There's no stain there."

"Tell that to the law. So you refuse to let me in the trunk?"

"You're damn right I refuse. You have no right. It's double indemnity—you're not a police officer."

That made me laugh so hard I started to resent that I could not like him even a little.

"Look—what's your name, fella?"

"What?"

"What is your name?"

"Jim," he said, slipping into his lot mode.

"Jim"—my diaphragm was in vermicules—"Jim, that's not what double indemnity means."

Now he was irritated again.

"Really? You'll find out what double indemnity is. Judge Hamilton Swiggum is a family friend. I'll take this up with him this afternoon."

"Right. When you see him, tell him to be sure to come down and get his sticker."

Jim put the car in gear but kept his foot on the brake.

"You know, I could just as easily go to another filling station."

This induced me to a galloping chuckle.

"You'll find out how funny you are."

The car still didn't move.

"How?"

"What?"

"How will I find out how funny I am?"

His expression changed suddenly from exasperated to con-spiratorial—a white Rolls had just pulled up behind him as if to make paltry his career. He was going to try to charm me.

"Look," he said, "you and I both know this is a joke. Nobody with a body in his—"

"Or blood."

"Nobody with blood or a body in his trunk is going to pull up here and ask you to find it. So let's just, you know, work around"—here he actually *winked*—"this situation. I'm late for work as it is."

I cast an impatient glance back at the Rolls.

"Sir," I said, "I find your refusal to permit the search of your trunk suspicious in nature. And I feel compelled by honesty to let you know that we have been instructed by the police to report anything vehicularly suspicious direct to them post haste, without delay, and right away. Now, if you don't mind, we have another customer waiting."

"Assface!" he called me, and as his car lurched in a screech onto Fourth Street I determined that next time I was about town drunk I'd seek out his car and piss with vigor into his exhaust ports.

I semaphored the Rolls into the vacated spot.

Mitzie rolled down her window and the vapors of a whiskey wafted into my face as I leaned on the door frame.

"So early in the morning, Mrs. Skumsrud?"

My eyes lavished over her morning dishevelment, the dress that had left the bra out all night open to the sternum so I could see the complete profile of a breast shaped like a tiny cornucopia that reminded me a little of one of Jim's ears. The other breast pointed at me like a finger in a coat pocket trying to be a gun. The fur coat that fell off her shoulders gathered again to conceal the ghastliness below her waist, stockings torn or missing, twisted garters, snaps snapped and unsnapped.

I marveled topographically at the contrast between stark sternum and concertina of neck flesh. Another long night keeping her soggy head off bar tops had passed, and the morning brought a hasty application of lipstick like an egg sliding off a piece of toast, and green and bloodshot bedroom eyes like to hell with the coffee, and somehow Mitzie and I perpetuated a secret correspondence in which pity gave way to an abstraction of lust and strange mutual regard.

"Why you impertinent boy," she said, in no particular hurry. "I thought I might stop to pick up one of those stickers now in fashion. Would you like to check my trunk?"

For a brief moment we were complicit in search of a lost double entendre.

"I'd love to," seemed the honorable thing to say, and she handed me the key.

Stacked properly, nineteen Evelyn Hartleys could have fit in her trunk, but it was as empty as a suicide's chateau.

"You keep a clean trunk, Mitzie."

"When you get to be my age, you have to."

And that should've been it. I fixed a sticker inside her windshield. Mitzie Skumsrud's car was OK, and the cops would have to look elsewhere for their killer.

But she didn't go anywhere. She stared at the sticker.

"You want any gas or anything like that?"

"I must look terrible," she declared, turning to look me square in the eyeballs.

"Mitzie, you don't know how to look terrible," I lied, for she was quite expert at it, and when she didn't seem immediately appeased, I added with frail exuberance, "And one of these days I'm going to dive into your private dishevelment with all the devilment in my bones."

She broke from her trance, laughing in a way I must still have been too young to decipher, and responded mysteriously, "Oh yes you will," tossing her thin skein of red hair with just enough arrogance it seemed not to matter whether it wound up in the back seat or not, and driving off then, with a sticker in her window and what passes for dignity in a small city when viewed from behind.

Wearing down, but in no way lacking in confidence I was headed back into the shop, in fact had just managed to caress the door handle, when a two-toned car of old and indeterminate make double dinged to attention. With the sigh of a thousand working stiffs, I turned about to face my duty.

"Gas or sticker?" I asked the driver, a skinny man with jaundice skin and eyes that skulkily refused to engage mine. He was hunched over the wheel as if he expected I would try to snatch it from him. He jerked his head toward me, managing to mutter out of the passenger side of his mouth, "Sticker."

"Here," I said, handing him one while trying to fit the rest in my back pocket. "You put it on."

He drove off fast and was replaced before I could reach the door.

This time it was a family man, wife in front, four boys behind, their chins on the front seat. Well? Did daddy kill the babysitter or not?

"Out of stickers," I said abruptly, and went inside where Stella was behind the counter with her feet up and her skirt, consequently, down (in the sense of up) around her hips.

"Honey," I said, "I just can't take it anymore."

"Someday," she said, looking a smoldering cigarette butt over adoringly, holding it like it was a bullet removed from her own arm, "they'll invent a filter you can smoke," and she dropped it on the floor.

"So," she proceeded, "you think you were friendly enough to grandma Skumsrud?" She watched her thighs curve tautly to her knees.

"She's still an attractive broad."

"Sure, if you like them balding, bony, and…and…"

"Bedridden?"

"Boozy!"

"Bored."

"Banal," she said, rhyming it with canal. "What a wreck!"

"You're too kind, Stella."

I leaned against the counter between Stella's legs, facing her. She dug her heels into my thighs to draw herself closer, the chair feet scraping the floor.

"You work too hard, baby," she said, taking note of the weary expression on my face and perhaps the car that had just pulled up.

"I'm doing the work of two men."

She looked a trifle bored.

"Two men!" I screamed at her.

The goddamn car out there was honking, too.

"Two men!" Stella screamed back.

She had as lovely a spirit as ever I saw in a broad.

"It's not glamorous, Stella! You think so at first what with the ritzy broads and the puke on the running boards, but you wake up and look around and it's just another inside of another dirty trunk."

The metallic beast out there was honking like a wounded pachyderm. I could barely stand it.

"Shitbirds," I said. "As if a human being is likely to respond to that hollow tintinnabomination."

"Well this human being," stirred decisive Stella, "can't stand it and would rather respond."

"Then go, tell them to get lost. No more stickers. A girl is dead and they want stickers!"

"What if they want gas?"

"No more gas."

"Oil?"

"No more oil."

"Okay."

Off she went. Back she came.

She clambered back and climbed the counter and wrapped her legs and arms around me from behind, warming her brisk, chill face against mine.

"What did you tell them?"

"I said the cops had a suspect in custody so they called off the sticker business."

Her lips nibbled marmotlike at my cheek.

"Don't go to school today, baby."

"You know I won't."

She ran her fingers through my hair. She had a delectably faithless air about her.

"Did I keep you up too late?"

"That or I work too early."

"And two jobs at once—it can't be easy being both a cop and a gas station attendant."

I relaxed back into her, absently snapping the elastic of her socks.

"It's not sane what they're doing here, Stella."

Steve, Oct. 27, 1953, Evening

I'll tell you exactly what they're doing. They're screaming their innocence like a fucking hanging party, meaning you have to have exactly everyfuckingbody in on it. Not most of the people, all of the people. Everyone in the city. The entire city is fucking innocent. This they need to do because everybody is fucking guilty. They built the city to protect us and their days are constructed of fucking ritualistic prayers to the city—have you ever fucking thought of that?: every fucking rev of every fucking engine is a fuming fucking orison to the phansigars of the fucking future, the formicants, our fate. And this advanced fucking elaborate fucking protection scheme, this monstrous extortion, has clearly been revealed for the sham it is. It's fucking defective. It failed to protect a 15-year-old babysitter. They botched the baby sitter job. What good is a civilization if it can't keep its well-adjusted middle-class babysitters alive? Why leave the deserts and forests? What have we fucking gained? Factories?

Fine! We exchange factories for protection—but the protection isn't fucking there. We've come in from the dark fucking ages, and instead of wolves and big cats it's people stalking us, and if it's citizens killing citizens it's fucking back to the fucking beginning. My old man, that good-for-nothing fuck, told me one thing my whole life that was worth repeating and that was someone should go drill a hole in my head so some smart guy could shit in it. Our civilization needs to have a hole drilled in its head so some smart guy can shit in it. Instead what the fuck do we got here? Nothing but looking back and forth shrugging shoulders and cringing in complicity: you didn't do it + I didn't do it = we didn't do it. Look who they already arrested and questioned—that salesman from Eau Claire and the negro drifter. It'll go on and on like that, wait and see. The city isn't working, but only because of evil forces outside it, from the country, the woods, the wicked thicket, where Satan resides. What we need is more fucking city. "The lawless functioning as forces of disorder always harbor grandiose desires for order," wrote Mumford. Read your history. That's how it works. That's what's going on here.

One-Arm Buzzy, Summer, 1953

A 15-year-old girl doesn't know what she wants, I told Bobby that straight to his smartass face.

I could have predicted he'd laugh at me. I swiped the crowbar from him and worried the drawer of the register a while. When I get mad I got to do something with my hand. Sometimes I think he made me mad sometimes just so I'd take over for him, whatever job he was working on. That's not to say when it comes to tools I can do more with one hand than he ever could with two. It gripes you to have someone stand around and watch you and gripes you to stand around and watch someone else. I don't know what to do about it, except get used to it, which I never can. One thing about Bobby, though, is if it's quiet long enough he won't let that silence stay empty for long.

"This one does."

He had to say that right when I almost had it, but the crowbar hadn't bit and when I pushed once hard my fist slammed into the register window and cracked it.

"Oh, horse cock," I said.

He took the crowbar from me.

"Hold the goddamn thing," he said.

I give the machine a pretty good squeeze, even with the glove on, and Bobby got her pried open pretty quick.

"Count it," I told him.

"Buzzy," he says, "you gather the money, take it home, and then you count it."

"I don't want to leave room for disagreement. Count it."

Nothing'll drive a crowbar between folks like money.

"How about if I just count the bills."

He was about on the sixth 20 when I thought I'd mess with him.

"Never mind," I said. "It's against the law, anyway."

He lost count.

"Goddamnit, Buzzy, I know it's against the law. That's why you should let me count it and get out of here."

I waited till he was about the same place.

"Not this—the girl. She's jailbait."

"Fuck!" he cursed, and began stuffing the bills in his pockets.

"Go fill a sack with beer, Buzzy."

"Get the quarters, too, at least."

Bobby, Summer, 1953

"It's just a quarter, Millie, for Christ's sake," Stella said.

"A quarter is a quarter," the apparent Millie said.

Stella already had my attention with those first words I ever heard her speak, but it was her next few that won me over.

"No," she insisted, "it's not."

That did it. I was in the booth behind, facing the opposite way, my back to Stella's, and I had been reading a book, *A Farewell to Arms*—Pilar, thou placeth thy thingeth of thy donkey in thy crack, no better not say crack, in thy spaciousness, is the cave where thou hath hidden thy rope-soled sandals—so I hadn't been paying any attention. But now I turned and propped my legs along the seat so I could lean back and watch.

"Oh really," Millie said, inflecting her sarcasm towards me, having caught my eye and assumed I was on her side, where all the logic was. She was a real dirtbag, that much was clear. "A quarter is not a quarter."

"Right. It's a little metal disc or one fourth of something, or in the case of a horse the whole thing. To say a quarter is a quarter isn't necessarily true, and it's no reason to stiff a waitress."

What Stellaquence!

"I'm not stiffing anybody. I don't have change. Besides, I don't owe the bitch a quarter."

"Yes you do," I said, figuring by now it was my turn. And Stella turned and I saw her face for the first time, her brown eyes and their incandescent malice, or, if she chose, their penetration, or range of sexual inflection. The girl was remarkably expressive in the eyes, which were in part orchestrated by her lips, also highly motile, wry, removed from their circumstance in order to comment on it, as she did when she looked at me without surprise, without haughtiness, restraining her interest by tilting her head slightly, narrowing the focus of her eyes, and turning up just one side of her mouth.

"What's your interest in this?" she asked. "You married to the waitress or something?"

"Up to now my interest was you, but I see you're a little young."

"A little young for what?" she said archly, broadening her smile to include me in the ambit generated about her lips.

"Good point," I said.

"Adele, let's just leave," her friend said.

"Stella's not leaving 'til you slap a quarter on the table."

"It's Adele, not Stella," she pointed out, yet continued as if I truly were speaking for Stella, "and she can stay here all day as far as I'm concerned."

She stood up and paused expectantly.

Stella ignored her, remaining turned towards me.

"I'm Stella," she said. "What's your name?"

Bobby, Summer, 1953

"Hey, Bobby," he yelled over to me, "This 'frigerator's got nothing but Walthers!"

"Cheap shitheads in every way," I said, coming up to Buzz. "That's why I came to work for you. Now let's get out of here. Stella's waiting for me at home."

This was too much for him, even from me.

"She's there now? Already?"

"What do you mean already? I told you we met this afternoon."

"It's a *school* night."

"I doubt it."

"You picked up a 15-year-old at the diner and you're already keeping her in your bed all night?"

He made no move to clear the beer out of the refrigerator; instead he stood there looking at me with his face exploring modes of disapproval. I had my pockets stuffed with cash, and intimations of daylight were harassing the recesses of my mind.

"You going to get the beer or what?"

"I'm not drinking *Wal*thers."

"Then let's go."

It was a cold morning for summer, one of those presages of late October in the middle of July, the pre-dawn sky dull and cloudless, without stars, without promise of sunlight or warmth or intellect, suffused by the lonely aspect of myriad attenuated conflicts of spirit, of memories of the failures that would be announced by dawn. I was reminded again of my old boss, Vernon Skaff, whom we had just robbed, that prick, forcing me to open his goddamned gas station every morning at four-thirty, his leverage my financial need. For the first time his money felt good in my pocket.

Buzzy's getaway truck was six blocks away, at Second and Division. *I* drove so we could perpetuate the fiction that he was just along for the ride. We cut behind the brewery and made our way down Second Street without detecting any signs of life.

"Do we ditch the glove?" Buzzy asked once we reached the truck.

"No, we take them down to the cops."

The escape route was an elaborate swing through the downtown, up to and around the university, and back to my place, where Stella would be under the sheets, a pert yet languid idol of flesh at whose feet we would count the money.

"Well, where, where do we ditch the glove?"

"Jesus Buzzy, we'll fling the gloves out anywhere, one at a time so they can't match them up. I mean mine."

He gave me a kind of pouting look.

"Wait till we're through downtown."

"Right."

The only life downtown was breathing out bubbles of poison phlegm on the sidewalks, face down or propped against bar fronts, sprawled in alleys, skulls topheaving off benches, all once men, now solitary ragdolls with their shirts untucked to expose gray slabs of flesh drowning in flesh. All they had wanted was for someone to touch that gray flesh.

"From all over Europe they came to forge a new life free of the bonds of tyranny, to freely practice the religions they just weren't all that good at…in rope-soled sandals they come…"

"Who comes? What are you talking about?"

"People passed out back there."

"What people?"

"Christ Buzzy, all over downtown."

"I wasn't looking."

"Well it's no different from any other night."

"What's wrong with it?"

"Nothing. Nothing is wrong with it. It just marks a strange phase of our evolution, a sort of cul de sac of human endeavor, as Steve would call it."

Buzzy rolled down his window, pressed the fingertips of his glove in his armpit, extracted his hand, grabbed the glove, and flung it backhand out the window. We were at West and Vine, entering an enclave near the university. I tossed my gloves out at 13th and Vine.

"Maybe they'll blame it on college students," I said.

"Say, what about that teenager of yours? We're not counting the dough in front of her."

"We might as well. I already told her what we were doing."

"You, not we."

This seemed an odd time to stress that.

"Right, what I was doing."

Then it seemed to dawn on him what I said.

"You *told* her?"

He looked like he would weep.

"You told her? It'll be all over the high school tomorrow."

"She's not going to high school tomorrow, it's summer. Besides, she's the kind who knows how to keep her mouth shut."

"I don't like it."

I didn't respond. I felt like a tube of walrus shit.

A few blocks down 16th he said it again.

"I don't like it."

This time there was an edge to his voice, a flinty sound, as if the words resonated against their need to emerge.

"All right, Buzzy, I'm sorry I told her. It was wrong."

"You shouldn't be playing around with a 15-year-old girl, keeping her out of school."

My only answer to that was back in my bed with Stella. It was something I could smell, but not something I could get across to Buzzy.

"I don't like it," he said again as we pulled up in front of the barber shop. Upstairs we could make out Stella's silhouette, wuthering back and forth.

"If it weren't for the money I wouldn't set foot in there."

"Then we'll count the money right here."

"Somebody could see us."

"Then you'll have to suffer my moral indiscretion. In the flesh."

"I don't like it."

"You don't say."

As soon as I opened the door Stella bounded up wrapped in her ghost sheet.

"Did it work? Did you get away with it?"

I smiled like a savant pleased by trinkets and watched her little shoulders try to disappear under the sheet.

"I'll tell you right off, Shirley Temple, I don't like this," Buzzy griped from behind me.

Stella stepped aside so she could see him.

"Don't like what?"

"You and him."

"Me and him what?"

"You 15 and him 30."

I had eased away to let them go at it and now I watched Stella's face brighten into a laugh that seemed to trace the room like the brief life of a celestial mishap.

"You just robbed a gas station, for Christ's sake," she reminded him.

Buzzy looked like a man who'd just discovered his shoes were on the wrong feet.

"So," she said, inviting him into my apartment, "shut the door and come in and count the money and try to be nice."

Bobby, Fall, 1953

The second and last time I saw Evelyn, her appearance set off a spat between Stella and her friends. Stella was of a race of fast and daring young girls, lawless subwenches who did as they pleased, courting their oppressors in order to defy them. They often got thrown out of eateries. Evelyn on the other hand was of the elite sect of wealthy, proper, tall, lithe (or fat, pimply and *really* rich), beautiful, obedient girls whose futures were charted with dreamy precision. School broke down barriers only to reconstitute them using more durable materials. The wealthiest of that clique was Magdalena Skumsrud, daddy's girl. Evelyn, daughter of a mere college teacher, was the poorest. Still, the economic gap between Evelyn's people and Stella's was multidimensional, unmathematical, and its defiance, therefore, by the mysterious bond between Stella and Evelyn, all the more disturbing an affront to the girls who fit snugly and content on their own sides of the line. That such a bond existed there is no doubt, yet so impenetrably were the two tribes circumvallated, Evelyn and Stella could do no more than exchange precociously sterile pleasantries that Evelyn's side iced over wordlessly and Stella's side derided, at times savagely.

I was the only one at our table paying any attention at all to Evelyn before she left. I watched her, across the diner—Shimshak's on West Avenue—eating her salad with impeccable forksmanship, her knees interlocked with those of what could only have been an aunt, a sort of arid underfleshed type who was expert at makeup, from the rich side of the family, reserved, decent, capable of unloosing a shitstorm of propriety behind closed doors. I suspect women like her of harboring envy for girls like Evelyn, purely physical envy, which they exact revenge for by little degrees of training in the etheries of life. Not to say Evelyn was a great beauty, and she had none of the adult sexuality of Stella, but she already had nice hips, the hips of a mature, slightly large-boned, woman. She was wearing the red jeans that would become infamous, the death jeans, as it were. Her breasts were hidden by her sweater, a yellow, ribbled thing she wore to please some younger cousin who gave it to her for Christmas last year, or for her fifteenth birthday. She was a girl who could not fail to display an inner complexity that was her recourse with the exoteric; she had the repleteness of being of a middle-aged woman cuddling a single drink early in the evening in a quiet tavern, face in a limbo between dutiful and shades shy of preoccupation. Evelyn's matronly escort held a small purse she unclasped gingerly, her elbows praying-mantised on the table, and produced a five dollar bill she handled as if it had just been cleaned and pressed.

Wending in file out of the diner, Evelyn and her aunt passed our table and when she recognized her schoolmate, a brief and charming wonder registered in her eyes, something yet short of warmth.

"Hi Stella," she said, without breaking stride, without smiling.

"Hi," Stella said, attentively, a little vole up from its hole.

"Hi," highly chirped Molly Bott in mimicry.

"What?" Stella said.

"What?" Molly aped.

"So you're friends with *her* now?" Randy Shifter rhetoricked. Randy Shifter was the undisputed maven of Stella's coterie. As Stella once said of her, she put the dirt in dirty blonde. At 16, Randy was already two years dropped out of school, had cultivated a network of devoted thugs, and was beginning to develop a moral code that she was smart enough to use to enhance her authority over her friends. Molly Bott was the only one who could have beat her up, but she was a loyal lieutenant and would not. Randy's curt pronouncements generally closed a discussion. Molly probably didn't even know who Evelyn was.

"What's wrong with it—she let me copy her tests in math. She even went out of her way, pushed her test so I could see once she saw I was copying. And she never said a word about it."

Dark, languid sluttrix Gabie Mansur was waiting her turn.

"So *what*," she summarized nastily, snapping that *what* like a whip.

"That's just the way good girls condescend to us," Molly Bott explained.

You didn't want to be a good girl around this coven.

"She's a stuck-up bitch," Randy Shifter pronounced, and all expected the conversation had ended. Later Stella said she probably should have kept her mouth shut. I rather hoped she would. I tried to avoid socializing with Stella's friends, for what I would sooner or later realize with a sharp pain in my spine like a pair of tremendously strong bony hands just snapped my head back into place was that I was spending my time with a bunch of teenage girls. One was okay, three was chronic. Worse yet, the mind thus squalidly pent will unaptly wander, and I did not enjoy harboring gross lusts for that tough blonde superslut Randy Shifter, who was not above giving my leg a little rub under the table, or the occasional demi-furtive ball squeeze whilst Stella was off in the toity powdering her keg. Such, though, were the rules, that Stella be allowed to parade her conquest before the girls. Our contract was simple: on these very occasional occasions I could be as quiet as I wanted but was not to appear bored, and if I absolutely *had* to leave the code was Did anyone else hear that Eisenhower got shot today? Or Nixon or Dullard. An assassination, anyway. My rewards for good behavior were considerable.

"Bullshit," Stella said, a shockingly direct affront to Randy Shifter's authority, a veritable uprising.

The ambit of our round table was briefly charged with anticipated melodrama. Girls do love their blood.

"None of you know her," Stella continued. "I do. Of course she isn't friendly to you—she's got friends we hate. She lives in a different world. But that's just a matter of chance. When it came down to it, she helped me out, and had it been any of you she'd've helped you, too."

Later Stella explained to me that what she couldn't stand was Randy having to pronounce judgment when she obviously had no idea even who Evelyn was. If she had just teased Stella it would have been all right. But calling someone a bitch who helped her cheat was wrong.

"Why don't you go and hang out with *her* then," Gabie Mansur said dryly.

"She'd act a little different if you actually wanted to hang out with her," Molly Bott elaborated reasonably.

Randy watched her minionettes work.

"I didn't say I want to be friends with her," Stella argued. "I said she isn't a stuck-up bitch, which is true."

"She ever invite you over?" Molly asked. "I mean, after one of those math tests."

"No, but neither did I."

"The problem with you, Stella," Randy finally said, "is that you'd rather be one of them bitches, but as it turns out you're too much a slut, too stupid—especially in math—and too poor. You're a nobody going nowhere and we're the only ones who don't mind. Until you start showing your true feelings, until you let slip deep down you think you're too good for us. I agree with Gabie: Go try to be that bitch's friend. You'll come begging to us."

"I wouldn't beg a whore like you to kiss my ass," hot little Stella told her, to avoid having to respond point by point.

That was where I came in. There was no time for code, Stella was about to get slapped in public—at the very least (the knuckles of Randy's fork hand were bony white), and if that happened I'd have to defend her, which would mean the wrong kind of contact with Randy, and likely before long someone like black-haired, acne-scarred, leather-jacketed, motorcycle-riding, switch-blade wielding moron-devotee Vic Veglan.

"What Stella means," I thrust betwixt, "I think is that you're all acting like a bunch of high school girls, which if I get you right is about the last thing in the world you want to be. Even if you are. Who gives a bald rat's ass about the true nature of some passing starlet. You're bored, girls. All of you. You need to do something, pay a little more attention to the outside world, maybe. How many of you know the President of Venezuela had a hemorrhage today? Read the papers"—I extended my hand to my princess, who was rising with baited eyes, trusting my instincts, but still pissed off and looking for a place to get cornered so she could lash out again—"come with me."

I had her out of arm's reach before Randy could react.

"You're lucky," she said to Stella, "I don't steam little bitches in front of their boyfriends."

"Maybe next time," Stella said over her shoulder.

But of course, next time things were different.

Chorus, Girls

When Evelyn was lost we saw
That little girls are made of straw

Their tender flesh that grew from seed
Could vanish, evil bloody mead

Amniotes and lambs eat oats
The barns are red with feeding goats
In rut and bleating obscene quotes
Of little girls in bright red coats

California, Illinois, Illinois, Illinois
California, Illinois...

Todd Mills

"What's that postcard?" Adele asked, for she could see it sticking out of my shirt pocket.

I had forgotten it was there. I found it in a copy of Lewis Mumford's *City in History*, which I purchase often at used book stores. I may have read it five times, or I may never have finished it.

The book comforts me. One of the finer slices of my daily life is the half hour or hour before work I spend reading at a bagel joint.

That morning I found a postcard in the Mumford book. The front of the postcard was an actual photo of the empty crown room, part of the main dining room of the Hotel del Coconada. The lights of chandeliers suspended from a vaulted ceiling formed crowns. The photo looked as if it were a black and white that had been touched up with colors.

The place was swank.

On back I saw that it had been mailed from California (it was made at the Actual Photo Co. in La Jolla. It was "Finished in West Germany." A copyright was included.) to Larkey Family, 2805 E. Kenwood Blvd. Milwaukee, Wis., postmarked July, 1975. I had grown up a short walk from that address.

"Dear Larkeys," the script read, "plans have changed. Will arrive in Milw. at 3:56 p.m. Flight #414 UNITED AIRLINES August 1st (Friday). See you soon, Love, Frankie."

The proximity to my childhood home, of course, made this an interesting artifact. I did not know a Larkey but was even more intrigued by the combination of the Dear Larkeys with the "Love, Frankie."

I had the eerie sensation of simple pieces madly disordered. One hears about strange communications from distant states. I knew a woman in Iowa who was visited by an obsessed admirer, who came all the way from Phoenix on a Greyhound to see her with no plausible hope of a friendly reception. Her landlords shielded her, and eventually the police were called to escort him back onto a bus.

Evelyn Hartley would have been a prosaic 37 when Frankie sent that postcard.

Again, I felt the chasm in me open at the baffling passage of time and the impossibility of reconciling the witnessed, or captured, portions of lives we have come across with the enormity of the rest of these lives, that exist outside our purview, like untamed beasts, or the persistent conclaves of the dream world.

I suppose the swoon is caused by the quick alertness to the insufficiency of consciousness to abet the understanding of life we somehow come to feel we owe ourselves.

Newsmen record facts. Old-fashioned newsmen try to interpret them.

Evelyn Hartley was taken from the Rasmussen house by someone who tried to enter through a bedroom window, then found a basement window, accessible through a window well, that couldn't lock because the catch was warped. He entered, then, through the basement.

Blood outside the house, blood spread over against the next house, suggest a terrible wound, Evelyn fighting for her life, attempting to flee to the neighbor's house, where her killer caught her again.

The evidence of a desperate struggle coupled with the silence in the neighborhood—a few blocks away someone thought they heard a scream, but the immediate neighbors, who were home at the time, heard nothing—brings on the same queasiness I have been trying to describe.

Is it simply the need to know? Puny man in the giant universe seeking answers. I don't think so. I think it's that consciousnesses interact and give each other the sensation, if only on the subconscious level, that, like Evelyn making her desperate dash for the neighbor's house, that without the available language with which to do so we are trying to communicate and receive communications. The sense that this is going on and that we are helpless to even glimpse this desperation sickens us.

"It's old," Adele said of the postcard. *She* was a prosaic 37 that year. "When I lived in California I ran into a guy who grew up in West Salem. I don't know what he was doing out there. We met and had a conversation in a bar. Naturally Evelyn came up when we found out we were about the same age. His name was Bill, not Frankie, so you can rest easy about that. He said he had a younger sister. And one day, one night, when he was about 12 years old, he was left home alone with his sister. His sister was younger. His parents went out late. He was in bed, he said, and this was not too long after Evelyn was killed, and he felt like as he had been left alone with his sister he was the head of the household.

"After they had gone to bed he heard a noise downstairs in their house. He said it was the kind of noise you hear as opposed to the kind you think you hear, the kind of noise that could only be made by someone moving around. He could picture the intruder having knocked something over standing perfectly still, waiting to see what would happen. Bill waited, too. Nobody moved. No more noises were heard. Bill either had a knife by his bed or in his room, or he bluffed it. But what he did was, since he took very seriously the responsibility of protecting his sister and therefore had to take some kind of action, he got up and quietly descended the stairs, listening the whole time. The intruder was still in the living room, and there was a swinging door between the living room and the bottom of the stairs, and when Bill reached the bottom of the stairs he paused to gather his courage, and then he said very deliberately, remember he was only 12, very earnestly, 'All right. I'm coming in and I have a knife.' And he went through the doors and no one was there. A clock, or some knickknack, or something had fallen on the floor, by itself. He searched the house anyway, especially since he was both relieved and proud by then. He said that was when he felt like he became a man.

"Quite a story, isn't it?"

Marla Rothgert

A red wave crossed the parallel.

At night the dream continues after you wake up looking for its shards. Wide awake in the furry dark the dream goes on and on and on. Next to you, still as a corpse, the body could crumble to dust, crumble to dust.

Tom Gerard

I guess you could say it was my first sexual experience.

But I don't think you could call it a homosexual experience. I don't think I even knew at the time for sure what it was. He put his hand on my leg and I got out of there. He took me in the back room—I honestly don't remember even if I was buying condoms—he took me in the back to show me some magazines. Only afterwards when I heard everybody talking about Heinie Schmock did I realize he had a reputation. Before that I had no reason to pay any attention when his name came up.

When you're that young a lot of what you do is by instinct. I think it was by instinct I knew something was coming with Heinie. I have no recollection of ever being warned about that kind of thing. Girls were warned to stay away from strangers, but boys were supposed to be able to take care of themselves.

He was pretty old then, so I suppose it's possible the same thing happened with my father, that he was the first to, that he did the same thing to my father.

Stella, 1963

Look at my legs. I've always had good legs.

I was with Bobby all the time, from the day I met him. The first night we made love and I didn't go home, we didn't sleep, he robbed a gas station, I met his best friend, I skipped school the next day…or maybe it was summer…

I took him home to meet my mother, who was so indulgent, or realistic, she gave me prophylactics by the dozens which she bought from that old pervert Heinie Schmock, who of course never laid a finger on her. Heinie Schmock was the first person to make a sexual approach to my father—so my mother said. So my mother bought prophylactics from Heinie Schmock and I always had some in my purse. The one night I didn't see Bobby, the one night in all that time I can remember, I had to use one of my own. But of course I had plenty. He was playing poker and he wasn't sure I should come along. I wanted to, but we had only been together a week or two, or a month at most. I thought I could bar hop their table or something. I wanted to. I had a brother who was a runner at the biggest game in town. It's in my blood. He hesitated, so then I thought I should just stay home for once, read a book or something; believe it or not we didn't have a television. But I got bored and went to the diner where I ran into some friends who were going to the pool hall on the north side. I must have known something, as they say, because I just happened to be wearing my sexiest dress. You know everybody wore wool skirts and they made every girl look the same. We had a waist and hips, that was it, all of us, all of us girls with interchangeable legs—that's how you knew we were girls. Not that you couldn't find a way to make yourself stand out—I knew what I could do with my eyes, from the time I was 11 I knew about men and what I could do with my eyes. A very handsome man at the pool hall looked at me when I came in, and he looked at the others, and I knew how to look back, and I looked back again after I walked past him, and I smiled. I wore my red and white gingham dress, a hand-me-down from my sister, who was a waitress and was a little smaller than me all the way around. The dress was very tight and I pulled my underwear up tight, I liked it to climb up because I knew men liked that—women and their goddamn girdles, they're so stupid. From kindergarten on up boys'll do anything to see our underwear. And that dress was so tight my hips and ass expanded into it like a long breath, and this Portuguese man, very beautiful, I still remember his name, I can still see him watching me. I suppose I was already as fond of my boyfriend as I could possibly be, but Lewis was beautiful and as frank as I was, so even when he said to me, You have great legs—he could see them from almost the knee and I moved around so he could sometimes see more, and when I sat even more—he said You have great legs, you're the kind of girl who will always have great legs, I knew it wasn't just a line. Yes, of course, he was trying to pick me up, but he meant it, too. It was true—he could have chosen any number of lies if he'd wanted.

He was Lewis Lomba, born in Lisbon, Portugal, and he had lived in just about every city on the Atlantic coast: Buenos Aires,

Sao Paulo, Bahia, New York, Boston…Lisbon—Lisbon's on the Atlantic. He was 28, and he had come to see the Mississippi, where he lived on a houseboat and fished for clams. He said it was easy. He was in Lake Pepin most of the summer, a shallow lake, and all he had to do was walk on the bottom feeling the clams with his feet. That's what he did for a living—he walked on the river bottom. Lake Pepin, and now he was trying Lake Onalaska, which is why he was down by La Crosse, they're both actually part of the river. Sometimes he found pearls inside the clams the size of marbles—if he was lying he would have said golf balls. Besides, I think he showed me a couple of them. And he told me all this in bed, afterwards, and I was asking because I didn't know about clams and I thought maybe my boyfriend and I could try it the next summer. Japs made buttons out of the shells. Lewis said he'd be gone and he could give us a few hints.

Lewis Lomba. Lomba was his last name. What I loved most about him was how involved he was in everything he told me. He had wonder in his eyes all the time. Though I only knew him that one night. In August, I think, and he said it was getting cold early that year, that it was going to be an early fall, so he was going to New Orleans next. He didn't want to see me again. Without telling me I knew how he felt. When I talked about my boyfriend, he felt it was all right to have one night with me, without guilt, without talking about it, but we wouldn't see each other again even though he'd still be around another week or so. Exactly the way I felt.

He told me he saw a spoonbill, a huge prehistoric fish with a paddle for a snout. Someone caught one in the lake. When he asked what it was he kept talking to people about it and heard all kinds of stories, like that there once were so many of them in Lake Pepin you could cross the lake on their backs. I never told Bobby about any of this, of course, but one time I just told him I heard there used to be so many spoonbills in Lake Pepin you could walk across the lake on their backs, and he thought that was just hilarious, but he told me that since the lake was only 20 years old, created by the dams they put in the river, the fish must have just died off recently.

I don't think Lewis believed the story anyway. He was just fascinated by the fish itself, and then the idea of how many there once were—there must have been a lot more at one time, at least. He said he'd seen a lot of dolphins, and sharks. And we were on the river itself, in his narrow bed, and moonlight frittered across the water, a natural light in the night I could see his face by as he talked. I was on my elbow and he was looking up at the ceiling, sometimes out the small window the other side of him, and when he looked at me, it was me, who he had just met, it was still me and not some trollop he just fucked. He was a good man. I was a trollop he just fucked, I was, but he didn't see it that way and so I didn't have to. He was wild, but in the finest sense. He was a good man. I knew even then I wouldn't want to keep him, at most see him every year or two, for a night…listen to his stories…

The houseboat would lift and settle back down again, not rocking, it would lift now and then, you could hear the water fold over itself where it swirled against the pontoon, always the sense, if not exactly the feeling, of the water moving under us, all the way to New Orleans where he was going, and I had no illusions, just the romantic feeling, as beautiful a man as you could ever see, and adventurous, me and my notions, not childish at all, thinking of this man who was so much like the river—it wasn't childish because I liked him no more for the fact. Nineteen-fifty-three. I understood him. I felt like you do when it's the right time to look at the stars with the grass warm under your back. It's not always the right time. I talked about my boyfriend and Lewis said he sounded like a good man, as if he had known me long enough to give me advice, which I listened to like he was my brother. But we laughed about it, too, I'll admit that. Fucking was light, a light thing, he said, and I knew what he meant. My boyfriend would think of me while he played poker all night. He would miss me and think of me, I would be alive as an image in his mind, not fucking a Portuguese vagabond, but the same girl nonetheless—Lewis had a way of putting it that was beautiful, cheating even was beautiful because it was true, and my boyfriend was honest and loved me already, had already fit me tightly into his life, a 15-year-old girl, as if it were the most natural thing in the world. I wouldn't tell him I two-timed him, Lewis agreed, and he told me stories about women caught cheating, one story after another as if he were walking me through the night on the backs of spoonbills, that's how wondrous was the night to me, story after story, as if the history of the world was nothing but women caught cheating on men and what happened to them. Not that he was moralizing—remember he was stroking these legs, that's how true he was, it really was my legs he liked most, and he touched me everywhere, when he touched me between my legs I jumped like a fish he said, but the whole time we talked he stroked my legs, or the leg at least I had thrown over his stomach. It's just that he seemed positive it was best not to tell my boyfriend. And the first stories were cautionary, but soon they were just the next stories that came into his mind, one after another, you could say like a river swirling up to the pontoon, forming an eddy of rising water that would fold on itself, only to rise again, and fold, without monotony though, one story after another, as natural as can be. The funny thing is that I can only remember one of them. I think even the next day I could only remember the one of them. Probably because it was the most exotic. It was in Brazil. Probably a lot of them were in Brazil, and after a while now I remember I was on my back with my legs apart a little, and he was up on his elbow, his free hand stroking my legs, and while he told me stories occasionally his hand would touch me between my legs—it was just natural—and I would leap like a fish, it felt so sudden and good, because I was two people, a body being played by his hand and a mind listening to him talk, and without realizing it I was eager for him to touch me between my legs. But the one story I remember his hand was still, or so great was my concentration I was one person, my body oblivious to his hand, probably, probably that story meant no more to him than the others. He heard it in Bahia, which is on the coast of Brazil where he lived for a year, working as a stevedore. He heard a lot of stories there. This one was about a man who became a monk, a wandering monk and then a rebel who was crushed by the government. But the thing is he was born into a rich family and they found him a beautiful wife from another rich family. The two families had feuded long before—no, they had been feuding for a long time and his marriage was the end of it or was supposed to be. A reconciliation. They didn't live in Bahia, they lived in a wild mining town in the backlands, which Lewis said was like our Wild West, a lot of gangs, wandering outlaws hired by one rich family to wage war on another. These two families had been at war for generations, but there was a lot of pressure from the government to end it as the country grew more wealthy and tame, and more companies from the United States and Germany wanted to invest. They couldn't have so many outlaws running around, so many wild towns in the interior. So they settled it by marrying the son, the religious fanatic, to the daughter of the rival family. It seemed everyone was happy, everyone was ready for peace. And many peaceful years passed. I can't tell the story as well as Lewis. But many peaceful years passed. And this son, not yet a religious fanatic, he was a lawyer, and he traveled a lot, and one day his mother visited him and took him aside and told him Son, I regret to tell you this but your wife is having an affair. If you don't believe me make an excuse to leave town only don't leave—go and come back and hide with the house in plain sight and you'll see what happens. So he told his wife he had to go to the coast for business, to Bahia, where he often went. He gave her plenty of advance notice, so she could make her plans, and when the day came he rode out of town, and when night came he snuck back and hid watching the house, cradling his rifle in his arms. They all had rifles and they could all shoot, Lewis said, it was the code of the backlands. Jimmy Stewart wouldn't have lasted ten minutes in the backlands, Lewis said. Even John Wayne, someone would have shot him in the back. Anyway, so this lawyer has a rifle in his arms and he's watching the house, waiting and waiting, shivering in the cold of the night until finally, at midnight, he saw the figure of an outlaw, in an outlaw's hat sneaking up against the house in the moonlight, toward the bedroom window, inside which his wife is obviously waiting wide awake with the light out. As the outlaw started to climb in the window he fired once and it went right through the back into the heart. Then he ran into the house and shot his wife right between the eyes. Only then did he check to see who the outlaw was, imagining it was one of his family's rivals. But it was not. It was his own mother, dressed like a man. She could not stand her son being married to the enemy. So horrified he ran away and over time became a monk and went crazy, without ever knowing the full story, because his mother never told him what happened to his real father, her first husband who he never knew about, who was shot climbing into the window of the wife of one of their enemies, who was the girl's father, and who shot him. She believed he was murdered, ambushed on a trail and then taken to the enemy's house, where they later made up the story that he was shot trying to get in the window.

I know that's confusing, but that's the story Lewis Lomba told me the night I cheated on my boyfriend in his boathouse, the story I remember, men or mothers dressed as men climbing into windows after women and getting shot, one of the men the wife of the other, killed by the son who went mad. A few months later a man climbed into a window and took Evelyn Hartley.

The next morning I did a strange thing. I hadn't slept. I said goodbye to Lewis. I threw my underwear in the river, out the window, facing north so it was swept from my sight before it went under. Then I put on my gingham dress and I walked home, all the way back to the southside, at least three or four miles. I missed my boyfriend and I hoped he hadn't called for me at home, I hoped he played poker all night and won a lot of money. I knew I wouldn't miss Lewis Lomba, but I also knew I wouldn't think up a lie, I wouldn't be afraid of my boyfriend if he found out. But he never did find out. And I couldn't tell you how many nights Bobby and I stayed up all night talking, sharing cigarettes. That was the thing about Lewis, was he didn't smoke.

Todd Mills

There are dead hours in an afternoon. It was that way even before electricity, before fluorescent bulbs and humming appliances.

I've often imagined happiness as the condition of never being aware of the need to kill time.

Adele Markham was smoking a menthol cigarette, and I wished that I could still smoke. It would have been just the thing to go with that rank coffee. She sat and smoked and looked across the room or at the window. She was in no particular hurry to tell her side of the story.

That living room had the feel of a motel room, something decorated for you by someone who didn't know you, a pretty arrangement where everything expendable inside you could live.

Yet I had no desire to return to the office, and as usual I had my home life blocked from my mind. That's how I've managed my life. The hours allotted to work are absolutely devoid of family, and as few as possible of them are devoted to work. Most days a reporter's job can be accomplished in about a third of the time designated. Some of the spare time must be spent appearing busy at the paper. A great deal of it can be spent killing time.

Some days I would go to the university's library. I'd get out of the car and hear a voice from a noir flick in my head: They'd never think to look for you here. Which was true. No adult in his right mind spends his free time in a library anymore.

It was a long time ago I had heard about the Hartley case and went there one afternoon to the university library and read the papers on microfilm. I remembered the bungling investigator Adele mentioned, toting his lie detector test like he'd invented the thing. I remembered a picture in the paper of a boy being given the test, seeing his head from behind, his crewcut. He looked like he was 8 years old.

And I remembered the little bit of physical evidence that was actually reported. Those tennis shoes with wear marks that "may have been" caused by operating a Whizzer motor bike. I had to ask someone what a Whizzer motor bike was. Good police work. Everyone who ever owned, borrowed or rode a Whizzer motor bike within so many miles of the city was tracked down and interrogated.

They found the shoes by the highway between La Crosse and Coon Valley, in other words out in the woods. Nearby, near the shoes, a jacket was found, a denim jacket. What made the jacket suspicious was that it was within a hundred feet or so of the shoes, off in the woods. One trouble was that the shoes appeared to have been tossed in rapid succession from a moving vehicle, while the jacket was too far off to have been tossed from that same moving vehicle. More troubling was that the shoes were size 11, while the jacket was quite small, perhaps a boy's jacket, far too small for anyone with size 11 feet.

Luckily, a smudge in the blood on the Rasmussen house could have been made by denim.

Special Investigator Schmidt had the jacket analyzed as carefully as the shoes and found that wear marks on the jacket could have been made by the kind of leather contraption a steeplejack sometimes wears.

No mention was made of a blood stain on the jacket.

Steeplejacks were tracked down and questioned, but of course you can't find all of them.

What began to become interesting was the simple question of how many people were involved in the murder and abduction. Police are notoriously close-mouthed about evidence in these cases, but quite often they let slip the singular, referring, for instance, to the window he tried to jimmy before he found the one that wasn't locked. Clearly, they believed they were looking for one man, not both a Whizzer rider and a midget steeplejack accomplice.

Scanning through the 1953 and 1954 papers I watched a separate drama unfold, behind the scenes, as local authorities gradually came to realize that the man they hired to crack the Hartley case was, in fact, insane.

Schmidt wanted to apply his lie detector not only to likely suspects brought in for questioning, but to *everybody* who conceivably could have killed Evelyn Hartley.

And then the steeplejack. If one man acting alone killed Evelyn Hartley, either the jacket or the shoes had to be eliminated. Prints matching the shoes were found between the Rasmussen house and the car, ergo the jacket is out. But Schmidt had fallen in love with his steeplejack theory, the way the leather belt fit the jacket with the neatness of a genuine clue, and he could not bring himself to give it up.

Before long it was clear that Schmidt was going to become an embarrassment. Local cops were quick to realize that the only thing Schmidt had that they didn't was that machine. A few months into 1954 I could see that he would have to go. But I never found the article. The Hartley stories occurred less frequently, and when they did, as in *Montana Man Questioned in Hartley Case*, Schmidt simply was no longer mentioned.

Peter Kurten

I left home on a week day, about 9 o'clock in the evening, putting the hammer in my hip pocket. By the Residenz theater I met a young, slim girl, who later told me her name was Dorrier. I asked her to come for a walk. At first she did not want to. In the end she went with me to Schumacher's. We went by tram to Grafenberg and walked along the banks of the Dussel. Dorrier was on my left. Suddenly I gave her a violent blow on the right temple. In order to do so I stepped back. Without a sound Dorrier collapsed. I grabbed her wrist and dragged her several metres from the path. I then used her sexually, after having pulled off her knickers from one leg. I then gave her more heavy blows with a hammer on the head. After the first blow she didn't say anything more, but only groaned. I took off her cloak and also the hat which was very bloody. I hid these things in the bushes.

Steve

Heinrich, dumbass, it's short for Heinrich. He's not a Jew, he's just a fucking German.

Bobby, Oct. 24, 1953

All the world's a dance, if I remember my high school Shakespeare right; and all the night is its choreography, albeit spontaneous or nay be it foreshadowed or shortened—I mean to say it's a sort of, if I remember my high school French aright, it's a sort of bal des inertes, a nearly static, grand dance, a slow waltzing of the globe and we the lice upon her—I mean to say, I knew soon Buzzy and Sissie would drift away a few feet, far enough for Stella's memory to return, and she would belt me a good one or two, half serious, and then a song she liked would come on the Wurlitzerhundt and I would refuse to dance and off she'd go with another, and Buzzy's lone arm would be Sissie's umbilicus whilst he and I had an adult chat about this or that, and the rest would depend on the timing: Watch for Mitzie to head for the head.

"**Ernest**," the judge said, and for a terrifying moment you felt the egg of cosmic mystery beginning to crack, "**I would like a tumbler of the Elixir.**"

Elixir was code for moonshine, which is illegal, of course, but a place has got to have it. There's stills all over down in Crawford County, but the Coo Coo Club, I happen to know and the judge doesn't, gets its moonshine from a bottle of passable whiskey to which is added a third grain alcohol. It's the most expensive drink in the joint. The weird thing is the judge paying for it—paying for anything for that matter. He lives out in the country past Tumbleson Falls, in the only house on Runingen Place, and it's his ritual to drive home bar to bar, drinking on the house so as not to have to shut a place down for pissanty gambling or moonshine violations. The story goes he used to favor a place called the Ten Mile House out on Highway 14, and they had a lot of gambling there, and a little poison, and the judge would stop there and stay and drink all night and the judge can drink more than ten normal men, and the owner of the Ten Mile House just hated to give anything away free and couldn't stand the judge coming there costing him good money and generally making people nervous the way they are around judges in general anyway and this one in pregnant particular, and so finally asked the judge for money before serving him, and as the story goes the judge suddenly detected something malodious about the place and made a phone call and before the hour was up the place was raided, the owner in jail and later heavily fined, but the good thing about it was the judge learned it's best to spread himself around a little more, and that's not to say anybody's glad to see him walk in the door, but they find it easy enough to act like they are and the arrangement suits everybody well enough, though bartenders remain a little uneasy lest they be the man to give the judge his last tumbler of elixir before he driveth head on into some farm boy's jalopy.

"Don't think I forgot what you were doing when I came in," Stella hissed into my ear. I was looking off the opposite way, which seemed a reasonable strategy and so I kept looking off thataway until she slapped my shoulder a hard, stinging loose-fingered backhand that really hurt.

I expressed pain by sending a vowel up my throat after several garbled consonants.

"Christ, Stella!" I was a little angry. "I was leaning in close to tell her something"—I jerked a thumb at the judge—"I didn't want overheard."

"It looked like you were about to take a bite out of her tit."

"I can think of worse ideas."

"What?"

"She was getting on me about you and your"—here I whispered—"age."

"You're a lying shitbird."

"It's true."

"She had her hand on your pecker."

"She did not have her hand on my pecker."

"Bobby, I watched it, I walked in, looked around, spotted you at the bar, started toward you, and you leaned close to her and then right when I walked up to you and you were too busy to notice me she slid her hand up your leg. I *saw* it."

Stella had wisely limited her makeup job to some thick black paste meniscing above her eyes and deep crimson blood on her lips. Some women, you want them to eat you.

"What are you laughing at?" she asked, irritated at my self-impunity.

"I'm laughing, my little Dumky, at the extraordinary chasm between what you fear and what I feel. She isn't a bad tumble,

I'll admit that. But in my thirty years I've only met one of you."

I'll tell you the difference between a good and bad woman. When a good woman is mad she wishes she weren't. When a bad woman is mad she feels miserable but proud of herself and therefore glad. Now a great woman—she relishes the event for the phoenix of its aftermath. Right there next to the judge Stella had her hand where Sissie hadn't quite, and found herself the dolphin midleap to piscine zenith.

"Barmitzvahed again, you're going to miss your train, that beard sister's weird sister..." I sang along with Louis Prima to make my little Stella happier still.

"That last part doesn't fit," she sniped, but at least we were off the Turner topic, and fortuitively, for Sissie and Buzzy, entwined so looking like a Siamese twin or twins was/were back en bloc.

"Say," Buzzy did, "who's the broad that sings with Louis Prima on this? Sissie says its Kay Starr, but—"

"Keloid Smith."

"Right—Keloid Smith."

"All crazy all the time!" someone across the tavern screamed in the thrall or grippe of some kind of primal Prima-love.

"Keloid Smith."

And again as things do in a bar events sped up and whirled, Sissie bending forward to reach across to Buzzy's money pocket—Buzzy's standard encouragement to fondling—reminding both Stella and I of her bosom, "You practically had your mouth in there," she hissed, punching me hard on the arm, Buzzy watching and laughing and knowing, Sissie fishing, Stella between plunges of pleasure preparing to punch again, and Sissie fishing out a bill, Stella captured and drawn to her man, Buzzy and Sissie turning in mini-phalanx toward the privacy of the crowd. I turned Stella roughly and backed her against the bar, beside the alpine oblivion of the Judge, before the disengagement of the bartenders, pressing myself into her. I kissed her the way you can only when you're telling the truth absolutely. Her lips darted left and right like cornered rodents, but they, too, I captured, and they succumbed to the truth of the situation and our tongues didn't stop moving until neither of us felt the need to express our gratitude.

Alas, though, we animals are condemned to conceive activity between copulations; Stella bit my lip and laughed, pushing me away, and asked me to dance when the next song—a country emetic about jambalaya and gumbo fillets croaked by aforesaid Kay Starr, a tiresome popular tune I forgave Stella for—perked the joint up another notch. I refused, and Buzzy refused Sissie, and the erstwhile harpies went off together, and Buzzy and I lifted feet to foot rail and elbows to bar top and drank shoulder to shoulder like men, talking out of the sides of our mouths, grumbling about the song and the way women are.

"That reminds me," Buzzy said, "I was in here earlier and you know who I saw?"

"What reminds you?"

"No, I mean guess who I saw."

"You said that reminds me. What reminds you?"

"Jesus, Bobby, can't you just for once ask me who I saw?"

"Are you saying there's a dearth of who you saw questions?"

"I don't know what you're talking about."

"Well it's your topic, so I guess we're up shit creek."

"There's a cliché."

"Touché."

"All right, but guess who I saw here earlier today."

"That reminds me."

"Reminds you what."

"What you said before—that something reminded you of something but you couldn't say what either was."

"I could've if you asked."

"I did ask."

"All right, then. I saw Joe Kneifl in here earlier today."

"Joe Kneifl? I thought he was in Florida. Remember they had that bash in here for him: *You'll make a wonderful stranger*—and he did, too. He was a beautiful stranger."

"Well he's back. I wouldn't be surprised if he showed up here tonight."

"So what happened to Florida?"

"Hemorrhoids."

"What?"

"Hemorrhoids. He got a chronic case and had to come back. He said he only had lousy jobs down there anyway, like tying mattresses. He couldn't handle even that. Especially with the hemorrhoids."

"I can't begin to imagine that formula."

"I'm going to go put that song on."

Which again was Buzzy's balletic bar timing at work, for he walked off like a bucolic dimwit stricken by prophecy, so I could sit on my stool and twirl in time to see Mitzie Skumsrud slanking from her stool, and Stella returned by tide and time preclipsing the arc of Mitzie's path to the bath, which as every time bisected a section of floor grated to release the blast of skirt-huffing air activated by a button pressed by Ernest's brother Tyrone behind the bar.

Tyrone stood belly up to the bar like a bank clerk fondling for his pistol, timing the blast, so that looking at his tensed still shoulders you could almost sense those lungs down in the basement building up their pressure—you had the feeling they were trained to wait for the precise weight of Mitzie Skumsrud's heels and her summer dress, and those unpriced pounds of flesh and angly bones, and no undies. The button—I've seen it—is golden, but I haven't seen the tanks, or whatever they really are, nor want to, for I see those rusted lungs I imagine you can stare at until you think you see the faint contract and expand of the living.

No undies. No undies and intent.

Stella came to rest and turned in time to watch with me, and "Tyrone, you asshole," I whispered in her ear.

"Tyrone, you asshole!" Mitzie wheened without conviction, flinging her weary contempt over the judge's head and working her hands like flippers to smooth her already dejected dress, all without stopping, so that the moment repeated was but brief, the implications fleeting like electricity in a fly, a weird moment of simultaneity, a town converged unknowing on a moment when the richest man in the city jacked in a fat pot with his fat forearms whilst his wife elsewhere, wind-whipped, slipped her bony sketch into our minds as if to refill the pockets he fleeced.

I stole a look over at the salesman, whose face I fancied was blanched into the shape of Mitzie's bony ass.

I nudged Stella and nodded toward the fool.

"A dollar he's gone before she's out of the toilet."

"A dollar he's not."

One-Arm Buzzy

Sure, I know all about Heinie Schmock, I go in there all the time. I don't know what the big deal is. It's not like you need two arms to fight the old geezer off.

Tom Gerard

My old man drank Walther's beer—there were always cases of bottles, empties, in the basement. He was the kind of guy who set up his own particular rules and stuck with them. You might not always know what went into the formation of those rules, but you learned the rules. It's like loyalty, and he was a loyal man, too. He drank Walther's and he gassed up at the same station every time and that's where he always bought his Walther's beer. Maybe he got the gas there because of the Walther's, or he drank Walther's because that's what his gas station sold. Most gas stations didn't sell beer back then.

I could be combining two memories here, but I don't think so. A few days after Evelyn Hartley disappeared we went to the gas station to get one of those stickers that said our car had been searched and we were innocent. The whole family went with my dad, I think to state that we all together had nothing to do with the case, had nothing to hide. I remember feeling a great deal of pride, though it's probable that I really had no idea why at the time. My sisters and brother were even younger, they might not even remember it...

My youngest sister might not even have been born yet, come to think of it...

...no wait...

...I remember that we got the sticker, but I don't remember the order of the events, but it doesn't make sense as I recall it because we got the sticker, and the car was searched—a girl did it, a cute girl, a brunette, she couldn't have been much older than I was, I was thinking at the time. But I didn't know her. I went to St. Wenceslaus that year, she must have been in Central...

...my dad didn't show much emotion in front of people, but he swore when the guy at the gas station said they didn't have any Walther's—and my dad never went there again, and that's why we went to that other station, where the high school girl worked, that's why we went there to get the car inspected. It must have been different days. That place didn't have Walther's either. Dad started getting it at the little supermarket on Farnam, which was closer to our house anyway. He died from a hemorrhage not too long after that.

Todd Mills

The room was a diffuse violet in the retreating light of mid-afternoon. I imagined for a moment that this woman who had locked her husband in the storm cellar had one optimistic day given some thought to this arrangement, this light and these chairs and paintings, these small wood and glass pieces of furniture. I never gave flowers to my wife—a bouquet strikes me as a hasty abuse of color to achieve a brief, deceptive, sensationless hiatus.

Larry, her husband, had usually appeared at the brewery in filthy clothes before a woman who worked a packing machine started taking his laundry home and cleaning it for him. A person could do that much without asking after his wife, without investigating his home situation, without alerting a social service agency.

After the meter reader broke the case, as it were, brewery workers came forth to bear witness to Larry's condition. Often, they said, he came to work with bruises on his legs. Even though it seems unlikely that anyone at the brewery would get a look at his legs—short pants, of course, were proscribed—the newspaper I work for printed these claims. The *Tribune* also wrote that Larry sometimes bathed himself at the gas station near the brewery, and that in exchange for this privilege—he did this early in the morning, before his 7 a.m. shift—he mopped the gas station floor. The anecdotes about Larry collected about themselves a dull outrage tempered by pity.

I repeat that Larry was a janitor at the Brewery.

"What about Larry?" I asked Adele.

She looked at me with a wry turn of her lips, then reached for another cigarette, lit it, blew an expression of smoke, and turned her lips again to make herself softer.

"I guess you don't want to hear about Evelyn Hartley anymore."

She meant this to be ironic, so I didn't respond.

"It's true I'm willing to talk," she said, "but you guys called me, I didn't call you. I mean the first fifty times."

"Have you seen your husband since you were arrested?"

"Other than in court?"

"Other than in court."

"No."

I could have nodded off. Perhaps I would have if Adele hadn't shot a curt laugh into the heavy tide of approaching silence.

"What's funny?"

I recalled tender, defensive days of youth.

But I recovered quickly—I'm a reporter.

"You're not going to...what are you going to write? Will you leave something out of the story if I ask you, to?"

"I'll write what the story demands...won't I?"

"There's just one thing you can't write."

"Then don't tell me."

"Promise you won't write this."

"I can't promise that," I lied.

"We weren't married. Larry wasn't even my husband. But you can't write about that. I just wanted to tell you. I mean, since we're having such a nice afternoon."

Steve, Spring, 1954

Who gives a rat's ass where Evelyn is? She's dead, everybody knows she's dead—I'm sick of her, sick of everybody talking about her. She was a nice little girl and a bad man came and killed her—Where you going, Larry?…Skittish pissant—who cares if it was a salesman from Eau Claire or a steeplejack from Memphis or a negro or a drifter or her goddamn hunchbacked homunculus Neanderthal priest! She's dead. Dead. Dead! You hear that Larry!—Where'd he go down to the basement? Why let it ruin your fucking life? Evelyn is dead. She died for sins of boredom or something. She died that we might fill our lives with her absence. No offense, Bob, but she died so that half a year later you could fill some of your desolate hours playing out a hunch. Call it a lark or a spree or whatever way you need to pretend not to dignify it, but she died so you could fill up a hole—that's why there's an empty grave, else you would have to look elsewhere. Well my old lady dumped me and I've got as big a hole in my life as anybody, and I'll be damned if I'm going to fill it up with a dead girl.

Bobby, Spring, 1954

"Fine," I said, "then I'll go with Buzzy."

The lesson here is never go to the Coo Coo Club in the afternoon. The place is a gloomy bait for the soul. Sometime in the morning this squeamish kid Larry earns a quarter or two for passing a broom and a mop over the floor and taking the chairs off the tables and placing them in formation around these tables now organized as if for a bridge tournament. Some additional specter or other—I rarely find out their names, their faces are without enduring characteristic—moves about behind the bar, occasionally retrieves an item from the basement—I'm convinced without feet touching the actual stairs—this, the tavern's secret hero, the munitions officer, who will first thing set a new bottle across from Judge Swiggum's seat. No one will notice when the kid leaves, only at some point you notice something like a scent he leaves behind, a musk of fear, his foreknowledge of the moment he lingered too long and got himself run out of there on a rail or beaten brutally by sailors; and then what's left is the day bartender, who invariably has a moustache and a pitted face, few words to spare, for imbedded in each word is a high quota of annoyance—he must conduct himself with a precision of distemper that comports with a code he must never reveal beyond its suggestion that you, his customer, are in violation of it. Of course no sunlight is allowed into this bar where age is revered by indifference and youth tarnished by age—the wood of the tables and chairs and bartop are all preserved by the liquor they absorb along with the nightly laughter, bitter retorts, harmless lies, labyrinthine thoughts of opportunities hidden or squandered, pacts arrived at too swiftly for the new protocols they demand, all the curves of night calcined or reflected, the teeth and the bottles of one bar's containment of chaos. If a chair in the Coo Coo Club could talk it would groan under the weight of the twin buttocks of rehearsed hope and fickle despair. But under the observation of the day-time the chairs are silent, serving only to deflect, or calcify, the clarity of sound issuing from the bar, where our dour diplomat with his moustache and his pitted face banks ice cubes into a heavy glass tumbler so the whiskey he pours sounds like an alpine cataract, explaining just that simply our presence in a moment in space and time, every fifteen minutes or so, and that's all he has to say, that nothing is worth desperation, and we know he's right because he never seems to get drunk.

Last night Veronica Slade dumped Steve.

"I saw it coming from the minute I laid eyes on her. She swore on her mother—as if women like her have them—she was always honest about these things. Last night I walk in here and she's got her tongue down Joe Turner's throat."

All aspects considered, Steve was holding up quite well. He was out of the house, he was bearing it in public. He spoke evenly. Lesser men broke their backs on the love of Veronica Slade. To call her a vamp and a half isn't covering the truth of her. She's a frightening dame. I really only saw her once, right in the Coo Coo Club. She was leaning over straightening a stocking when she glanced up and caught my eye. I looked away immediately, but it was still weeks before I could think about another woman. Thereafter I tied myself to the mast the instant I sniffed her. You heard about the guy who said he touched lightning—it was a real thrill. I like lightning, I like it a lot, I like what it does to an atmosphere—but I don't want it to hit me. Not everyone's like me. Steve is the kind of guy who wants to know what lightning feels like. I looked at him across the table: now he knows what lightning feels like...and he's actually holding up pretty well...maybe I ought to reconsider my way of thinking...

"She's as amazing as you'd think, too. You always knew when she was near, even before you saw her. She's more than human. There are dimensions we don't understand contained in her."

Because it was like wind turning a close copse of trees, both men and women turned to look at her, I sprained my neck resisting. We were like monkeys when a tigress stalks by, no one need say a word...alarm and awe are in the air.

"I knew what I was getting into, and now that I got what was coming to me the only recourse is to go further in."

Steve is a mystic.

"I'm not saying she's not a bad woman—she's the worst. But more in the sense of a natural foretaste of apocalypse. She's a tornado, a poisonous snake, a very specific malignancy. She's preternaturally heartless, imperial in her indifference, impossible to turn away from."

Steve is courageous.

"I walk up to Joe and I look at her and say what the fuck is this, and Joe's all right, to be fair, he says it's his turn, and I hurt too much to laugh, but in a way, I've been laughing since."

For Steve, the affair with Veronica Slade was an experiment in power. He had to find out what happened to someone who touched her. He had to know what lightning felt like.

"I started re-reading Faust in the German this morning. Before I'm through I'll have a great deal more power than her."

And after Veronica Slade there was no one.

Over Steve's shoulder I could see the pale face of the sweeper boy lingering like a ghoul above the basement steps. I wanted to throw a lime at him, chase him away. I looked around at the empty tables, at the afternoon captured in the tavern. I looked back at the basement doorway and the ghoul was gone—just thinking about scaring him off did the trick. The bartender (moustache, pitted face) stood with his hand choking his whiskey glass, gazing at the bar like a man without regard for the evanescent. He stood there a hundred years ago and would be standing there a hundred years hence. If I saw what he saw, *his* tavern was suddenly crowded with revelers yapping in silent animato, outside of his time, outside of mine, a momentary bartender-access to the undifferentiated. Probably all he really saw was the inside of his own headache. A gloomy scenario requires a romantic interpretation at times, else too easily is the play given over to disaster. Veronica Slade *will* have the final word (unless against Steve, if he is right); meantime we may make much of our losses.

"...But Buzzy's working today, so I'll have to go tomorrow."

"Go by yourself, or with that chippie of yours."

"My mere mortal chippie is doing something."

"Then go by yourself."

Steve's eyebrows met half-way, and at the outsides they curved up like the flaps of a sting ray. A subtle contraction of the muscles about the sockets meant to make his eyes appear to be seeing worlds unavailable to working lugs like me.

"I suppose that would be a solution, but what you fail to understand down there in that superior hot hell of yours is the joy of sharing discovery, or at least sharing the search. More and more I find that the better part of life—shared hijinks. Know what I mean, Hermes Trismegeestus?"

"That's what makes you weak. Strength lies deep in the isolated self—"

"The frozen, hyperboreal, overcivilized, supranietzscheated, abstractificational, denuded/reconstituted self..."

"As you wish, but it's too late for anything else."

"Except to frolic in weakness, as you'd have it...and as come to think of it so will I, frolic in weakness before the consideration of death, to preconcede you a point, death, in the sense of looming..."

"Or as enemy."

"Death?"

"Yes."

"Good. That's good."

"No, that's not what I mean."

"What then?"

"The enemy."

"Right, I accede to your terms. I consider death an enemy."

"No. You still don't get it. I mean I'm going to defeat the enemy. You can't see it, Bobby, you haven't been where I've been. You look away while I look right at it. You look at it and concede. I look and say Fuck you, death. That's what you do with an enemy—you fight to destroy it. I've lost the first serious battle, with that bitch of death Slade, but now I know the terms, and I will not lose. I have sucked the essence from Veronica Slade, now it's only a matter of turning it into the elixir that fortifies my own essence. It's already there in my veins…"

"I see," I said. "That's good. Maybe now I'll be able to drink in the same bar as that siren without falling victim to seizures of panic."

Marla Rothgert

Form into curtains, form into curtains, at the Hall of the Mountain King.

Todd Mills

"You weren't married to him. And nobody ever checked your papers?"

"What papers would they check? I really don't know."

"If this checks out you're certainly innocent of spousal abuse."

"You're not going to 'check it out,' Todd."

"That's true," I conceded.

"One thing you may want to check out, Todd, since you're a reporter, is a tip on the Evelyn Hartley case that I've never seen mentioned in a newspaper story..."

The lure of Evelyn from her underground: the ethers of dead Evelyn refused to abandon us to this mundane afternoon. I looked at the little metal door to the fuse box next to the kitchen doorway. I'd been looking at it without taking it in, and now I fancied Evelyn calling from in there, which could only be the case if it wasn't the door to the fuses, and that's how the mind works sometimes, a stumble to epiphany, a madness clarified, Evelyn calling, the metal door, Evelyn calling from underground, through the tube, the pneumatic tube, Larry Browning's triumph.

"*That's* where the tube is." I said.

She looked at me, wonderingly, almost vapidly, and then she saw what I meant and she laughed.

"That's the fuses. The tube is in the kitchen. You want to see it? It's some contraption."

"No, no...I've seen them. Tell me about this tip."

"This is all Bobby's idea. See, the cops blundered at first, allowing a huge crowd to trample the crime scene, and I think they were criticized for this. After that, they became more close-mouthed and everything. All indications made public were that Evelyn had been taken south out of town, from the south end of town—follow me? They found shoes off Highway 14, and the steeplejack belt, and they found underclothes, Evelyn's panties and sox, I think, under the Mormon Coulee underpass. Even then they tried to be slick about it—they never said it was Evelyn's clothes, but the paper did this big thing on her brother searching two miles of underpass and ravine and such. I remember a picture of him in the paper looking like a miner. I think if it weren't Evelyn's clothes he wouldn't have gone on that quest. So that suggests Evelyn was stripped and her clothes tossed out there and then a flight south on 14. But then suddenly, after a few months, the cops started searching Levee Park—*downtown*. Why? The cops wouldn't say, but what Bobby figured was that some piece of possible evidence caused this shift of direction, or some kind of tip, so he thought, all right, the killer dumps her bra and undies at the Mormon Coulee Underpass—where they'll be *found easily*—drives out 14, where he tosses the shoes, coincidentally where some tiny steeplejack has shed his tool belt, and this is just a diversionary tactic. He dumped her somewhere else. He doubled back, say, and dumped her. In the river? The cops certainly looked there, and obviously didn't find her. Bobby thought the killer must have been smarter than that. A river is too unpredictable, she could come up any time, any place—that, and it would be the natural place to look. So he got a big map and he put his finger on Levee Park and worked his way out from there, soon coming on the marsh, not the big part of it, but that little sector of it that's between Levee Park and the northside and sandwiched between the Causeway and the River, where there used to be lumber mills. Could you get a zoning map from 1953?"

"I suppose."

"An old zoning map would show that almost all of the bottomlands and forest on either side of the La Crosse River, that whole area, even a couple small lakes Bobby said don't show on the map, it's all zoned for heavy industry. You see those giant Mobile oil tanks there on the left down the Causeway—that's just the beginning of it. There are acres of barbwired wastelands, and there are junk yards or salvage yards back there, and vast cemented fields, a whole marsh covered by cement."

"And you think Evelyn was buried there, under cement."

"It's a lot more likely than Losey Boulevard and State. I can't say who would have done it, or why, but politicians and realtors have several kinds of dirty secrets kept in that area, and let's say the investigation shifted to Levee Park because of a car, something to do with a car. If you were going to take Evelyn Hartley and bury her under cement in that wasteland you'd have to get there somehow, and as likely a place to park as any would be over there behind that little brick building on the north end of the park. Then you carry her across a short wood bridge and you're in some pretty wild terrain."

Bobby, Spring 1954

"It's like the moon out here," Stella said, which just meant it was getting dark and the unknown was stranger than we'd have guessed...and a lot more unknown was promised if we didn't turn back...and even if we did it would tail us from behind, a hovering, before we could get back across the river. A great hound howled. No, it didn't, but the trees were bare enough to rustle autumnally in the wind, and the wind *is* invisible and strange. I guess it also meant that the thickets were bare, the woods shallow—a strip of woods ran along the Mississippi almost the whole way, and then on the other side of the path there were marsh woods, willows and ferns and conifers, young cottonwoods, and we came across two deer that looked enormous in the dusk, they looked dangerous, and we could hear what seemed a threatening huff of exhalation through their nostrils. We were certainly no longer in the city. Yet, legally, we could have been cemented over.

I knew she wanted to head back. I stopped and I squeezed her and she curved into me and I felt her up and her nipples were big and sharp from lust and cold and when she stopped my hand going down her pants it was like a kick in the gonads. Never mind the circumstances, she had never refused me before. Never. Never mind we fucked just two hours before. Never mind she was scared. We're out there looking for red jacket or red pants or an arm sticking up from a pool of cement—those pools of cement in the marsh were like the fucking moon. What the fuck were they doing out there? It's the kind of situation you get this subterranean feel, almost like there's a cavern of pulsing truth beneath your every step, the feeling you get the instant before your intuition meets the fact that verifies its lurch into the unknown. It was pretty fucking scary for me too, but Stella sets me on fire and I've got my own private mystical beliefs, inchoate they may be, but along the lines of two of us against the whole goddamn spirit world, that if we hold tight no ghosts can creep in between there, no fear of death, no Vic Veglans from behind.

What happened began with a misunderstanding—a good thing, as such, to get it out of the way. The misunderstanding I mean. I'd had it with Steve, and I was just standing up when Stella stormed into the tavern and began abusing me in that way women have when they're 15 years old and blindered with anger.

"Where the hell have you been? And don't say 'right here obviously' because you know goddamn well what I mean."

I looked at Steve, who may or may not have been observing us scientifically or goethologically, alchemically…

"You asshole," she continued, by now having come to a halt an inch from me. "I waited there for an hour. It's two blocks away, you inconsiderate prick—the least you could do is walk over and tell me you're going to be late. Who's that?"

"That's Steve," I said. "He's an alchemist."

"Well he doesn't look like one," she said, though I was sure she didn't know what it meant.

Then of course she turned on Steve.

"What's your problem? You couldn't do without him for five minutes…What do you like, boys, invert?"

"Look, hussy," he said mildly, "keep it between the two of you."

"So," she said, turning back to me, "you chose to spend your afternoon with this prick after promising to be with me?"

She seemed to really want an answer.

"Stell," I said, "so far I don't know what you're talking about."

"What?"

"What are you talking about?"

"You were supposed to meet me at Danny's Record Shop at two."

"I was? I thought you were with your mom. I thought Danny's was Monday."

"You work Monday."

"I know. I wasn't sure how I was going to manage it."

"Really?"

"Really."

"Then we don't have to fight."

"No."

"Oh. Good. Let's go—they're still open."

It was that easy with Stella.

And it could be this hard: halfway to the door she turned and stopped and barked at Steve: "I still don't like you."

Steve responded silently, as if trying to blaze into her soul with his eyes.

And of course, the bartender never looked our way.

"What's his story?" she asked once we were outside.

"You know Veronica Slade?"

"Who doesn't."

"That's his story. She dumped him last night."

"What's that got to do with you?"

"I grew up with him. We were neighbors."

"He work at a gas station, too?"

"He goes to college. Sort of. For the last seven or eight years. Since the war, anyway."

"Seven or eight years? He must be a real genius."

"He's the smartest guy I know. We were at Iwo Jima together. He jumped on a hand grenade to save my life, only he dismantled it before it blew."

"You liar. You weren't on Iwo Jima."

"Actually, we were. Our ship stopped there after the war. They already had prostitutes by then. But only twenty men from our ship were allowed leave. Thirteen of them had warts on their peckers after that."

"You already told me this story."

"No, that was in New Guinea. This time it's Iwo Jima."

Thirteen had warts on their peckers after that. One guy, Eddie Frankel, a skinny redhead with a remarkably ugly face, with warts on it, from Akron, Ohio, or Acne, Ohio—"

"Last time he was from Topeka."

"Tulsa. He took me in the bathroom and showed it to me—we weren't homos or anything, but he took me in the bathroom and showed his long, skinny penis, all topheavy with warts. It remains the worst thing I ever saw. You don't eat well after a thing like that...So what's the name of this band again?"

"Gene Vincent and the Blue Cats."

"Blue cats? This should be good—I've never seen a blue cat."

"You'll like them. You'll like them or we're finished."

"I like them already. Anyone who doesn't like blue cats lives in a world without wonder."

"Well they're not like Frankie Loon."

"Nobody is. All I expect is they're better than Mozart. On a par with Brahms."

"Oh, they are. They're new. They're the band of the future."

"They'll be here Friday the 13th? It'll be the most important date in the city's history."

"Shut up."

"What? We can't talk in here?"

For we had entered the notorious Danny's Record Shop, where I had never been and where Stella had learned to smoke Lucky Strikes. At our left was a short counter and a blonde teenage girl with a face studded by defiant pimples, unbalanced by a busted nose.

"Terry, this is him," Stella told her.

"Booth four," Terry said laconically, "when it's free."

Past the counter were five listening booths, each about 10-x-10 with a 3-x-6 window intended to afford employees a glimpse of the refined behavior of their clientele, groups of whom were stuffed into the booths smoking cigarettes. Teenagers waiting their turn sacked the record bins like Cretan widows at the Red Cross warehouse. Terry handed a paper number to Stella that made her next in line for booth four.

"You're next," Terry reiterated. "Just have them leave the record in there. Everybody's listening to Gene today."

At an early age I found I had already outlived my pride, yet I was able to arrange the contours of my quotidian such that I was seldom pressed into the service of circumstances I wished to avoid. So it was easy not having pride. Principally, I never shopped with women. And with minimal labor I could forge a treatise that would demonstrate shopping with a woman—for shoes, say—would have resurrected my pride at the cost of equanimity and wisdom, leaving me not only with aggravation, but some irrelevant bimbo in a pair of new shoes as well. She would be wearing those shoes long after we'd made each other strangers. Her love would be developing corns and fungus and bunions—and like toenails it would outlive even her, in the form of those shoes, the kind of thing one finds at the side of the road long after…long after…

So I accompanied Stella into Danny's without pride. I accompanied Stella into Danny's for love.

God help me, I thought.

Stella put her hand on my ass and ushered me toward booth five. A scrum of her classmates across the narrow shop took turns acknowledging us with complexes of excitement bearing little variance. I wondered which one had a cop for a father.

"I can't believe you've never been in here."

"They got names for men that lurk in teenage joints."

"Like pervert?"

I didn't know what to do with my right arm as I walked.

"Yeah—like that."

Each booth we passed had at least five high schoolers afflicted with St. Vitus jiggling spastic in smoke. Outside booth four stood a tall youth with black hair combed back wet and biceps that made his arms look like two anacondas in peccarian symmetry. In the space of less than a second I thought of Lombroso, noticed his pug nose, and knew I'd soon find him a plague delivered to me special. He was directly in our path and clearly wasn't going to move. His eyes decided they'd rather look at me with defiance than at Stella with scorn.

We reached him as soon as I decided the initiative was mine.

We were about the same height, but he had the larger bone structure, significantly more muscle, and the unique raw meanness that can appear in mistakenly civilized youth. I was glad we were in a public place.

"You're in the way, shitbird—is there a reason for that?"

He didn't like the way I put the question.

"What did you call me?"

"Shit," I said, "bird."

As he lifted his arms, Stella rushed between us and I wondered what the biggest rodent was. The guy was a regular force of nature. About as intelligent, too.

"No Vic," Stella said. And I knew who I was dealing with.

The capybara, maybe.

Stella dragged me around Vic, who said, "I see you around you're dead."

I had to shake off Stella's frightened, incoherent protests to step back to him, but I could see enough of the future to know I couldn't leave it the way it was.

"You just threatened my life, asshole—that makes it serious."

"Consider yourself," he said (like he meant it), "a marked man."

Stella was yanking on me like there was some sort of message I wasn't getting, something only a furious tugging could get across.

Finally, I turned to quiet her.

"Don't worry, Stella, they taught me in the army to use a knife."

I watched her brief quiet struggle to keep herself from telling me I was in the Navy, then heard Vic tell me I'd better bring several knives, and I knew it was up to me to end the encounter as well.

"Several knives, then, maybe one for you pro bono," I said, and smiled with genuine affection, if not for him, then for the life that was so big and dumb it made us feel sad for ourselves.

We did not have to suffer the proximity of Vic's feigned indifference for long; his people soon emerged from booth four. Stella dragged me through the smoke that rolled out, plucked a 45 from a redhead who said, "Hey, Stella" and shut the door behind the last of them, a guy who could've been Vic's brother.

"That was Vic's brother," Stella said. "You're in some real trouble now."

"Did you bring me in here to talk about a couple of goons or to play me some blue cats?"

"Caps."

"Caps?"

"Look."

She handed me the disk. *Be bop a Lula!* was the song, and sure enough the band was called Gene Vincent and the Blue Caps.

There were three wood chairs in the booth. While I looked over the disk Stella lodged the back of one of the chairs under the door knob. I looked up from the vinyl wryly. She pulled out a cigarette.

"Got a light, Marlowe?"

I looked her over and flipped my matches against her chest.

She caught them, and read the box. "Buzzy's Skelly Service Station," she said. "What's it mean, 'service?'"

"In your case, Slim, it means realignment."

"Put the record on," she said.

The phonograph rested on a wood plank stretched across the back of the booth. The whole set up was quaint and rudimentary, the kind of place you knew would disappear and be remembered different from what it was.

I watched the disk spin until the words "Be bop a lula" made more sense, then looked back at Stella. She hung her coat on a nail above the window and pushed a chair into the corner.

"Well...put it on."

I dropped the needle.

"Well, be bop a lula she's my baby," the record said.

I looked around. Hiroshima and Nagasaki were still the only cities missing.

There were several more be bop a lulas, some followed by unusual declamations of certainty, the rest by the she's my baby business.

After that the song got down to specifics.

"Well, she's the gal in the red blue jeans—"

I lifted the needle and swung around to Stella, who had crept up right behind me.

"The gal in the what?"

"The red blue jeans."

"The red—well are they red or are they blue?"

"Red. Blue jeans are jeans only these are red ones."

"Can't beat that for detail."

Something was coming over Stella. She had a high tolerance for my derision anyway, but now it was as if she hadn't the least idea I was on a different course from her. Her eyes were liquid and shining, and her lips came involuntarily open to unloose a curl of tongue that played her upper teeth one end to the other, mechanical and openly obscene.

I dropped the needle—

"She's the gal in the red blue jeans

She's the queen of all the teens

She's the woman that I know"

—and lifted it again as Stella ran her hand under my shirt, up my back.

"So," I said, "this guy only knows one woman…"

Stella took the phonograph arm from me, dropped the needle back on the edge of the record and pushed me back towards the chair in the corner of the booth next to the door, gripping my shirt to keep me from falling when the chair undercut me.

Her eyes were like black flames in water.

"Take your pants off and sit down," she said, and when I did she lifted her skirt to show me she wore nothing underneath.

"Oh lush limpet lips!" I exclaimed. "Above and below!"

The percussive tapping of the back of the chair against the wall of the booth provided musical enough transition between plays of the short song until perhaps the fifth or sixth run when Stella left Gene Vincent far behind and the chair went into a gallop that was sufficient evidence of our lechery for the gathering crowd outside our booth and did not need the crescendo of Stella's oblivious moans for validation; yet in the end, eight or nine plays of the best song I ever heard accreting to indelible memory somewhere in the skull Stella squeezed in her hands, it was the chair that relinquished, falling silent before Stella's long moan—a declension of voice and lust to limp body that could not have been heard more than a few blocks away.

For hours afterward I was incapable of seeing people, and sounds reached me as if from a great distance, like so many palpable silences.

Stella, May 17, 1959

Kiss me—to delay the transmogrification of my scream, cover the tunnel to my 15-year-old lungs with your mouth, for nothing of mine you'll find has the savor of my silence when I am offering it only to you and I am, the same scream a witness heard from four blocks away and thought it was just kids fooling around and now six years have passed and my body carries the same scream I've grown so tired of without relinquishing my desire for you with your eyes shut because you're too honest to pretend dark stories don't pass through your mind when you kiss me, your eyes shut and you're looking down, your soft elastic face rising and falling with the limpet movements of your mouth, and swaying side to side, your head in the current, making it seem so easy to remain attached as if the current does not exist to separate lovers, as if it isn't final, so I imagine these new cracks at the farthest fall of your sad eyes spread like fault lines from the strain you suppress out of love and the meaning of dark stories. My secret is that each time I am 15 years old, though I won't say that each time it is you or that each daily manifestation of singular beauty—the sudden lush of lavender from a green bush (our last daytime walk in Spring), the oblique purity of ice dripping in winter rain (our coldest fuck), the smell of a damp locust grove on a summer night (new love, first love, love teeming into the world)—I don't imagine these sent to me from your oblivion, but I am 15 years old each time, the way you left me—born in May, I never had a birthday with you—and I'm still alive and your eyes are closed and your mouth swallows me at the axis of two screams. We both knew what the disappearance of Evelyn meant and I've been screaming ever since and we both hid for each other the same omen, dark green, the color of the nightsounds of an owl, which you looked away from because you saw its emergence in my eyes when a mood turned them brown to that green, or so I imagined for you had such confidence the way you moved in the world there must have been some reason your eyes could never hold mine for long. Maybe you didn't know it. Maybe you didn't know why or even that you did it, but you did, you always looked away from me like you knew this happiness was forbidden you, you smiled, though, you smiled from the moment I met you I made you smile and you never broke down and in pleasure you smiled—I wish you could see how many since have made it seem like agony—always smiling for me and yet you had the saddest eyes I've ever seen. I'm grateful for eyelids. I want no eyes to open on me unless they are as sad as yours, and none will ever be so. How long is that story? How dark? Your mouth moves of its own accord but I can tell your hand has been forgotten, useless to your story, resting beside my breast, where it stopped to rest or fear attenuated unto death, at first repulsion, this breast old enough to be a mother,

I will bear a monster this day, this nipple that lost all feeling after you will suckle a monster from this day, a nipple always erect but never eager, something rubbery and superfluous without my monster, that you wanted to touch for its part in a ritual you believe has succeeded in deadening it, as if the intimacy of your palm, as if the fury of your teeth could fail, as if the ritual could be accomplished without feeling, with dead skin. Feel my cunt, oh father, and moan, for a man must moan when he feels a wet cunt, and yes, half must be gratitude. Now dampen my nipple with your palm and see that nothing has been lost. You know the ritual that deadens. You knew it with instinct and so did I and maybe it's as simple as that, that's why we were perfect together, we didn't give a rat's ass for the formula, I didn't have to hold your penis in my hand that first night or the first week and tell you that it's mine, or have you say that's yours, we didn't have to pretend to destroy ourselves day after day because we really did it, each day I died with you, and each day you died with me, we didn't have to mark our territory with cute names, private language that would embarrass us in public, we didn't have to because we left nothing behind, each field we crossed we burned, we didn't have to test each other with other men and other women, I didn't have to flirt with handsome men for the gift of your jealousy and you didn't have to force my love with tantrums of jealousy, you didn't have to look in my eyes with our heads on the pillow and say mmm, what are you thinking and so I didn't have to begin sentences I was just thinking how nice it would be, we didn't have to hold a contest to see who could keep their rectum squeezed shut the longest nor have that horrible and self-conscious jocular conversation that means little more than isn't it funny how putrid our intimacy smells, we didn't have to evaluate and make tinkering adjustments like how long my hair or yours, which clothes, am I too prinked up, no cute shit like would you like me better honey if my tits ampled out of my dress like hers, would you love me more if I had more muscles, and explanations, my god, so you won't be mad at me really if I only explain, really, how nice, all I have to do is explain and then watch the interminable process of your face releasing its anger or worse yet the aftermath of concealed embarrassment or fear that you went too far, you never put me through that horror so you never had to hit me when I laughed in your stupid face, laughed harder still when your own slap sent you to your knees with your begging arms around my waist and your tears trying to lubricate my cunt, laughing so hard I could hardly get it out how ordinary your passion was, how precisely you were repeating the same scene the last fool who thought he was unique put me through, the only difference being each time I laughed harder and only the first time with a little bit of sadness, because I knew then more than ever what you took away with you, and maybe even more than that, let me tell you the truth, that though you could never be that fool, I could have gotten away with it with you if you were me, if it were you you would not have laughed, you would've been kind and you took my kindness with you, I could not be kind to those men who insisted on that ritual— except a couple times when they had money and I faked it as long as I could stand it which wasn't very long. And Bobby, how desperately they all want to marry, every one of them too chickenshit to bring it up as soon as they want to, so they try to wait for me to start hinting and I start counting the days and if I really like fucking them I'd try to fit my little hand over their big mouths, but out it would come, every gesture of defense seduced them, and sometimes I liked them enough to call them fools to their faces, because not one of them even believes in it, not one of them had the guts or soul to believe in something that required a tenacity of spirit, they couldn't believe in it and so wanted it all the more, and maybe the worst were the ones I broke who stuck around begging for more, as if they wanted to learn from me, always more fascination than pain in their eyes when I showed them with what easy venom I spit on their weak little lives, no woman would love them forever, sniveling little bastards, they were lucky they got five minutes of my attention and there would always be some dreamy bimbo they could get a year out of, sometimes even vain handsome men with power, even they could cry, though they hit harder and they tried to stick around because they were incapable of believing me, nobody talked to them that way, I tried to get it across to them that yes one way or another every woman talked to them that way, they just could not believe they couldn't destroy me, little midwestern nymph, little nothing tart, little talentless Natalie Woodnymph, every time I'd see them afterwards I could see their eyes looking at me to see if I was getting older, you'll get old you bitch their eyes said, but my indifference was always stronger and I could see them inside their own eyes, across a restaurant, at a party under somebody's rotting palm tree in a backyard that sooner or later fell into a ditch, they had their arms around my waist and wept tears at my cunt and begged me to get older, to become ugly and undesirable, all the while a blonde more beautiful than me would be massaging his crotch that strained so hard to wound me because as long as I laughed in his face he was my prisoner, I was the one he wanted to marry, to destroy, and he knew he could never accept that I was immune to that kind of revenge. I could always do with a little violence—such punctuation—just a little, though, a little blood on my tongue, I've fucked a dozen men I could have easily run a knife through if they forced it, but a split lip, once or twice a black eye, sunglasses for a few days, a lot of orange juice, and no pity, my formula for keeping the screams down all these years, once or twice nearly vomiting it up with I love you, choked on in a moment of weakness, for those words would have meant utter betrayal of Evelyn, who was, we both knew, killed by these men, whoever did it she was killed by stupid men, which meant something different to you and could be suppressed by me until you disappeared, and that's when I knew the scream was already there waiting from the night I danced alone in the Coo Coo Club with my dress shielding my eyes and my scream a secret comet two miles away, on the edge of town. Strange activities reported from the periphery, remember the Robinsdale Peeper, and a girl thrown out of a car—that was me, the girl thrown from the car, not the Peeper, that was me before I knew you, I never told you about that, first so you wouldn't make the right assumptions and then so you wouldn't get killed, for it was Vic Veglan—he barely stopped the car, actually he didn't stop the car at all, and he leaned over while the car was still moving, turned off Losey and I almost fell out then, onto Coulee, and he was pushing at me and I was holding on like a cat avoiding water, all this silent, his friends in the backseat keeping their mouths shut, watching Vic throw a girl out of his car because she had no interest in fucking him, him and his friends of course, because she was a slut, that was her reputation and there's no worse insult to a man than to be refused by a slut. Maybe I was a slut because I'd just turned 15 and I already knew how much I liked fucking, but if I was a slut I was a slut with discretion, not a nympho, and I was already bored by men. I cannot love because I cannot live outside myself, the interests of men bore me and make me scream. I looked at Vic's biceps at the pool hall—Schindler's—I watched them contract into boulders when he bent his arm and I watched the left one stretch when he took a shot, I couldn't help staring like every other girl at the perfectly carved chest that never seemed to relax inside his tight black t-shirt. He lost the game to Nickie Turner and flipped a couple dollars on the table without making too big a deal about it, without calling Nick a hustler, without foolishly demanding another game, and there weren't too many girls in there and he knew who I was and thought he knew all about me and it wasn't too hard for him to get me into his car. I was all sex until he stopped at a friend's house, and then another's and then picked up a case of beer from that place that had the drive up, Bluffside Tavern, and announced we were going up to the top of the bluff. By then he figured he had me and was putting on a show, ignoring me, talking like a hard ass to his friends, not that he wasn't but now he was a juvenile Humphrey Bogart imitation, and I was already bored with him, bored with the way he watched himself talking with me— he didn't want to fuck me, he wanted me to fuck him, and I still would have but he had to ruin it by getting his friends. So he got his friends and he got the beer and I said I live down by 21st and Park and I want to go home now and he ignored me. I said I live at 21st and Park. So what, he said, pulling out of the Bluffside, taking a right, to head up the bluff. I got to go home, I said. And he laughed and kept going, turned to go up the bluff, ignoring me, so I turned the wheel for him and got us turned into the oncoming lane—there weren't any cars that late at night, and Vic shoved me so hard I banged my head against the door frame, and I let out such a vicious stream of bile he concentrated on responding in kind instead of turning the car back around, and so now we were headed the right direction at least, away from the bluff, and unconsciously he turned onto Losey, and consciously passed Park, the two of us screaming at each other: mostly I was a whore and I don't know what all I said to him except what finally got to him, which was that anybody who wanted his friends to watch his body move on top of a woman had to be a homo and I don't fuck homos because I don't know where all it's been and that was the first time I laughed in an angry man's face and laughed harder when he was so mad he couldn't get the door open and was swerving all over Losey, slapping at me and the door, trying to get it open so he could shove me out, one hard backhand splitting both my lips, finally getting the door open and turning hard onto Coulee, my mouth shut now I was concentrating so hard on staying in the car and after two blocks he slowed almost to a stop and I screamed when I lost my grip and turned a somersault on the asphalt, my scream turned upsidedown, people running out of their houses—one of them Viggo Rasmussen I found out later—the tail lights disappearing up the block, somebody assuming the authority to tell somebody else to call the police, strangers asking me if I'm all right, stragglers coming up so someone could say did you see that, shoved her right out of a moving car, fifteen people standing around as I got to my feet, backed slowly away and turned and ran like hell to get out of there before the cops came.

One-Arm Buzzy

Sure you got your suspects, you can't live around a town this size and not know several retards or what Bobby calls the manchild, the village idiot or whatevernot. The manchild of Jackson is the one I figure, a guy in his 30s living at home, sitting on the porch all the time watching children going to school. Kids are like dogs, they sense a threat, and kids were scared of the manchild. But the thing is you can't, you just can't blame a guy, ruin his life without some kind of proof. Still, the guy rode a Whizzer, and I don't know the truth of it, but they say the guy was wearing new shoes right after the murder. And look at where he lives—same goddamn block practically. His house is right next to the shoe repair, the first house west. Go down his alley and cross 15th Street and that's Evelyn's alley, her back yard right there at the corner of 15th and Johnson. From the second floor of his house he could easily see into Evelyn's back yard. You can't just go and ruin his life, but I hope the cops checked this guy out thoroughly. A couple nights I got Bobby to come with me and spy on the guy, but nothing happened

and Bobby's heart wasn't really in it, since by this time he figured the body was in the cement desert and she was killed by
someone with power, someone in real estate most likely. Why?
Well, Mr. Smart Guy can't answer that. But I admit it's not the
likeliest way to find a killer or find out a guy is a killer, parking
outside his house and watching a couple times. We could see
he stayed up late, and we saw him moving back and forth in
his room upstairs, which like I said faced the alley. There was
a lamp up there he seemed to be leaning over. He would pace
a while and stop over the lamp, which was like a little girl and
Bobby would start whistling that song—I can't whistle: dee dee
dee dee, dee dee dee, dee dee dee, dee dee dee, dee dee dee dee,
dee doo dee doo dee doo dee doo dee. One time he sang it with
states, California and Illinois, I don't get it. He explained it's
what the killer in a German movie with Peter Lorre—he was
the killer. Peter Lorre whistled this song when he was stalking
his prey. What's that got to do with California and Illinois?

Steve

I don't see what's so hard about it, the town isn't that big. Find
out who was missing that night. Who wasn't home? Who wasn't
where he was supposed to be? They're doing the opposite, of
course, counting heads to prove it wasn't someone here. If they
did it the other way around they'd find the killer soon enough.

I'm about the right age and temperament, maybe it was me. My alibi is a lying spiteful whore, but no one's asking.

Mitzie Skumsrud

It wasn't that salesman from Eau Claire, that's for sure.

Gerard

Any number of profiles fit the perpetrator of this kind of crime. The manchild type of pervert is only one of them. You could imagine this big, half-retarded, inward looking man, manchild, developing a crush on a girl he sees all the time, someone who lives near her and sees her all the time. I used to walk by the house on Jackson where a guy lived with his family, a guy who rode a Whizzer motor bike. I don't think I was old enough at the time to think of him as a suspect, but when I looked back on it he seemed an obvious suspect. Rode a Whizzer, lived really less than a block away from Evelyn Hartley. I used to walk past there to go to Powell Park, and though I wouldn't go out of my way to walk on the other side of the street, if I thought of it I would. He never did anything to me, or threatened me in any way, but he watched me, with a kind of grim expression on his face. He looked a little unfriendly and I was wary of him. That was all. I have no idea if the cops checked him out. It's quite a coincidence, the manchild who rides a Whizzer sharing the same alley as Evelyn. What if he developed a crush and somehow let her know and she made fun of him, maybe giggled with her friends whenever he rode past on his Whizzer.

Stella

I still think it was her father. I don't see why no one is suspicious that he was the first one to find her, like at 7:30 at night or whenever a father's going to panic and dash over to save his daughter. She couldn't have been in the bathroom? I don't know why he'd do it, or how, or how he passed a lie detector test—but what do I know about lie detector tests, why should I believe whatever a lie detector test says?—maybe he had accomplices. It may be a stupid theory but I notice since he was cleared no one has been caught, either.

Bobby

Heckler, the realtor. Something to do with the bean fields back there. Buying up the bean fields. Is it outlandish to suggest that someone who publicly and obviously cares more about money than anything in the world would kill a girl to scare folks into allowing him to build a sort of circumvalence of houses between them and the wilderness of the bean fields? Is it any more outlandish than the disappearance in streaks of blood of a 15-year-old baby sitter?

Joe Turner

Obviously, some sick son of a bitch killed her, someone really sick. I'd check the loony bins within a radius of 300 miles. How hard could that be? Some sick bastard on a Whizzer. It's a wonder they haven't found him already.

Judge Hamilton Swiggum

He will hang here or in hell.

Sissie Turner

There must be some reason they're giving all those lie detector tests to the college boys. I think they got a pretty good lead it was someone who Professor Hartley flunked out. I think they're just checking the high school kids for show. They've probably got it narrowed down to maybe three or four people and they just can't prove it yet. You notice suddenly there's all this hubbub over the tests? Why is that? Why now? I mean why not right away or a week ago? If you ask me it's obvious they're getting close.

Al Patros, Sr.

I lay odds it was that sick bastard, Heinie Schmock. They ought to hang him.

John Hopkins

I think about it every night when I go to work. This time it was a high school girl, but maybe that's just because she was the most vulnerable at the time. The killer is still at large. I tell Maggie to make sure the windows are locked and not to answer the door, to keep the shades drawn. We even put newspaper over the windows in back. And I never go to work without checking the window wells down in the basement, because that's how the killer got in. Maggie thinks I'm overprotective, but nobody is safe until they catch the killer, that's obvious enough. One time I forgot my thermos and since I had left early I came straight back home and Maggie already had the door unlocked. I saw a car in front of the house that wasn't there when I left, and I could see the door was open and I got so scared I jumped the curb and ran into the house, but Maggie was perfectly all right. She met me at the door, scared I guess from hearing my car jump the curb. She just wanted to cool off the house, she said. She said whoever's car that was she heard them go into the neighbor's house next door, the Bucholzs'. I told her not to be so careless ever again and she promised.

Heckler

Every city this size has plenty of unsolved violent crimes. It's never a pretty sight when a girl gets killed, and all the less so when she's one of your own as we consider Evelyn. But you run the risk of making too much out of it. The police, in whom I have every confidence, are working on the case every hour of every day, and that's pretty much all you can expect. As for the rest of us, our task is to put this terrible tragedy behind us and continue the good work of building a strong and safe community for the future. My heart goes out to Professor Hartley like he was one of my own, but perhaps I'm not alone in suggesting he take a little time off, maybe take a vacation, and see if he can't make his grief a private matter. The newspaper could help in this by paying a little more attention to breaking news and less to things that have already happened. If the case breaks they'll have their story, and if it doesn't what makes them think this city should be any different from any other. Try Chicago if you think one crime makes this a dangerous city.

Maggie Hopkins

I'd like to see someone try and attack me. I got a knife here that's just itching to cut the balls off this pervert.

Chorus

The streets sink away from the houses like a black ravine under the black hands of hackberry and black locust trees meeting overhead without a sound or with the unsuspicious rustle of a feigned night sound like a footstep covered by stealth, pause, the stillness of the night its own beast, the demon never seen, with as many faces as there are victims of night, who inherit the city and all its black, black on the white houses at night by the railroad tracks that fail to insulate the city, the demon with more faces than there are ideas of Evelyn and her last night—we can all say she was buried under Losey Boulevard, yet each of us behind drapes we now close, behind newspapers taped on the windows as soon as the night after, each staring at the perimeters of our lights sees the shadow of a different face and the outlines of something black working with the intense compact complexity of a terrible insect, we see a grave, the black figure working in the dark, the limp body of a dead girl we stare at, unable to move, our eyes accomplices to murder arranged by our own design, staring and mumbling to ourselves "something bad happened."

Detective Lester Sorenson

We have no suspects whatsoever. We have several profiles, but no one who fits the profiles comes under suspicion. The plain fact is, we've not had a single suspect. Everyone we arrested was a long shot. The chances the case will ever be solved diminish a great deal with every passing week without a clue. We can't make this public knowledge, but the family certainly knows that when there's that much blood at a crime scene, there is virtually no chance the victim lived through the event.

That's the most blood I've ever seen. I've worked suicides and never seen that much blood.

Marla Rothgert

Wake up, the dream resumes with figures that loom dark in the dark room. The bathrobe is a monk with his head hiding in the trunk. Baby eyes in the ceiling look down at the tomb—the room's in the Hall and the room is a tomb.

Peter Kurten

In June 1913 I picked up a girl on the Brehmenstrasse and took her out on several subsequent occasions. One Sunday we went to a dance at Gerresheim. On the way home I throttled the girl several times. When she was scared I said: "That's what love's like. I won't kill you, though." After that she put up with it. We had sexual connection on a bench.

Dr. Karl Berg, student of Peter Kurten

The vagina was large and undamaged, the anus gaped wide, permitting the passage of three fingers, excrement and dried-up brown leaves were visible in it. The rectum was also obviously large, and when dissected was found to be 12 cm. in diameter. There were no wounds in it. Tests for spermatozoa were negative. My findings were as follows: A comparison of the autopsies of the Albermann child and Maria Hahn show a considerable affinity. Evidence of throttling could not, of course, be proved in the latter case, but the stab wounds were alike in both cases. Each body had stabs in the left temple. In the skull there were the same triangular forms showing a knife with a rather broad back. The largest stab, in the case of Hahn, was in the forehead.

On the edge of the upper end the impression of the back of the knife was quite visible, but below, instead of a sharp cutting edge there was a slight crumbling of the bone. The length was 14 mm., which shows that the blade of the knife was certainly not longer and only a little narrower. If one considers that the points of entry have an average length of 12 mm., the blade must have been about this width. The longest wound track in the body of Albermann was 12 cm. by measurement. In coming to this conclusion, it had to be borne in mind that the infantile breast gave way under the weight of the stab. The wounds on the genitalia of the Albermann child were serious, vagina and anus were torn, and in the vagina I found spermatozoa. It follows therefore that the vagina had been violated by forcible penetration of the penis. I was not able to prove spermatozoa in the rectum. The anus could also have been torn in the act of coitus. As far as Hahn is concerned, there were no traces of wounds on the genitals. The wide gaping of the anus remains obvious, even when one considers the abnormal width of the rectum. The presence of the dead last year's leaves suggests sexual connection with Hahn while she was lying on the ground. The gaping of the anus and the vital reaction of the sphincter muscle lead me to the conclusion of *coitus per anum*. Thus we have further analogy with the case of Albermann. Even so, this conclusion cannot be called anything more than a presumption, for the decomposition of Hahn introduces too great an element of uncertainty into the diagnosis.

Bobby in Love

I ran my hands up her neck, nesting my fingers in her hair, cupping the nether slope of her skull, her jaw hinged open—oh, did I know her, Horatio—and I brought my lips that short, stark distance to hers, listening for the saliva she swallowed that would precede the hungry silent intake of breath, the lupine contraction of her stomach, the pull of her thighs by the shrinking moon of her anus, offering me the trembly thought of her dehiscent vagina, our lips trapping us in the inanimate embrace of awareness, a lag of impulse, our lips forming a cavern for the transmogrification of the beast we formed, and we looked at each other between the timid suicides of our eyelids.

Todd Mills

I had been to the cement desert. One of those give it to good old Todd Mills stories.

Todd's not doing anything.

Fetch Todd.

Or: Fetch, Todd.

The city wanted to turn this vast wasteland (read: nature) into a park. Build a baseball park, a nature park, an amusement park.

Send Todd out there to look the place over, if there's a story we'll give it to Jocelyn.

At the north end of Riverside Park, nee Levee Park, with some landfill adjustments two monolithic constructions stand where the fish ponds used to be—the fish ponds that were dredged for Evelyn's body. (Surely there is no mystery there. The cops received a call: "Her body is in one of the fish ponds in Levee Park." They dredge, find fish.) Across the La Crosse River probably little has changed since 1953. The railroad tracks that once led to a lumber mill were in disuse then, as was the scale back there out of sight of the city. The place is a wilderness of modern ruins and bottomland nature. Photographs of tigers stalking Mogul ruins come to mind, though back there I saw only garter snakes slithering over metal hulks I couldn't identify. Dying ponds, choking in lilies, were circumscribed by marsh forest, lots of willows and cottonwoods. The chaotic and vast back yard of a steel supply company accounted for a great deal of the rusting objects, and probably the enormous wooden spools. A rudimentary trail parallel to the river followed a groove between river bank woods and the old rail line levee.

Objects corroded into useless assertions of permanence were strewn the length of the path like stones—a washing machine, sheets of tin, axels, generators, hubcaps. The cement desert itself was on the other side of the levee. From the trail it merely looked like a field of young cottonwoods and willows. Another pond or two, smaller ones, were hidden like traps in amongst the tallest willows. Beyond the desert, forming a skyline of inert force, squatted several gigantic oil tanks.

To get to the desert I had to turn where the steel supply company got serious about throwing up obstacles, including a large boat, and some tractors. I climbed atop another levee, then a few yards past the last of the ponds, and descended the levee into the desert. On my way down I passed a turtle on its way up. Suddenly nothing of civilization was visible. Young cottonwoods rising out of pooled cement blocked the view of the oil tanks. Downtown was less than a mile from where I stood, but I couldn't even see the two ten-story buildings. No buildings on the north side of town were visible either. Where the cement was thinner than an inch or so, the ground gave way like sponge. The swamp was reasserting itself through all but the thicker layers, places where the cement was pooled as high as my knees, sometimes higher than my shoulders.

I had the feeling of having come upon an abandonment perpetrated long ago, only a sense of the grandeur of the original design available, the architects vanished with their plans.

But I found no mummies, no silver tridents, no skeleton of a giant ape.

The place was a desert.

A swamp.

Nearer the pond the cottonwoods grew thicker, though none taller than, say, a plum tree. I walked into this mini forest and came to a clearing, a clearing with a soft, spongy cement floor. And I sat there, for a long time. I sat there feeling utterly alone in the universe, and happy for it, strangely happy, as if I had achieved a sort of grace normally reserved for accomplished yogis. My cement lotus was still at the center of a chaotic and dangerous universe and I was independent of time.

I can't explain the fright that soon came over me.

A desert irony is the infinity of paths available there for escape. I calculated the shortest route, around the pond, through some thick undergrowth, up the railroad levee, across a narrow tract to the trail—in other words toward the river without backtracking. Close to the pond the bush gave an impression of impenetrability that was belied by the sudden and bizarre hulk of a rotting white boathouse tilting on its pontoons like a message from Conrad. It looked as if it had been deposited by a flood.

I boarded the narrow, covered deck. The windows were covered with plywood. A hazard sign warned of unspecified danger. A padlock hung open from the door.

I had no inclination to enter, and had in fact turned to leave when the door opened, releasing a plume of remarkable stench, a solid odor of sweat, neglected skin and moldering fabric. The man who lived within this boathouse of malodor wore an undershirt, shorts and socks, all the color of a sparrow's chest. His eyes passed across me and chose to glance instead into the distance, yet I still felt them on me as a sort of wariness. Within those sockets I detected an odd combination of animation and vacancy, as if they had traveled to the limit of his neurasthenia and survived. Even in the sunlight he was like an animal crouched at the back of his burrow, awaiting the decision of the predator with instinct, rather than fear.

"You live here?" I asked.

He didn't answer. His mouth opened and shut as if he were swallowing, a gesture of impatience, I think.

Then he swung his head.

I took a step back away from his smell. His hair was wild, not terribly long, his stomach quite round. He was filthy of course, but the skin on his face seemed young. I judged him to be no older than 30.

I didn't expect to get a word out of him, but perhaps some latent reporter instinct required me to linger until I at least got some sort of signal of hostility or hospitality out of him.

I imagined the hostility might be conveyed by a sudden rush.

I took another step back.

"Interesting place," I ventured.

He worked his mouth again.

"How long have you lived here?"

"Two years, ya," he said with an eastern European accent.

He looked, even after this outburst, incapable of speech, and the words he uttered seemed escaped birds, flying indecipherable designs in a distance he saw as a gray shield, his mind grown blank to their mockery.

"I'd call that long. What's your name?"

"George, ya."

"My name is Todd."

This did not matter to him.

"Where you from, George?"

"Prague, ya," he said, which must have been the answer to my question, yet the effect, engendered by his posture, his inability to engage my eyes, the way the words were launched so as to fall around me, was that of something more coded, like the territorial grunt of a beast: I had the right to pass by, but I was on the verge of flagrantly lingering, and we two were not of the same pack.

So I got the message. Out of habit I said goodbye. I climbed the railroad levee, stopped and looked back and saw he had already retreated back to the doorway and paused in the fetid shadows to watch my departure.

I left him out of my story, which described the cement desert and surrounding wilds in one clause—a marsh wilderness, or something like that. I quoted all the people who wanted to make something of the place, delivering a dull, impartial, factual story.

I never told anyone about the hermit from Prague.

About a week after I wrote the story I went back out there with a loaf of bread, but the boat house had been razed. I didn't see a body. I imagine one of the interested parties in looking the zone over found the boathouse an unsightly hermitage and did something about it.

This needn't have anything to do with Evelyn Hartley.

Bobby, Oct. 24, 1953

The Eau Claire salesman might've made it out of there, too, had he not been in too much of a hurry. He started out rather adroitly, weaving through the crowd and the tables and had nearly reached the door when the glass he still carried alerted him to its fears of indiscretion or panicked like a rodent on realizing he was about to smuggle it out of its natural habitat. He actually stopped then, observing it with alarm, and the two of them, man and tumbler, stood isolated together, antipodes of shared alienation, as if he had not been sucking its lip with his lips. But this hiatus was brief. He erupted from the torpor with renewed panic, bumping blind through the last of an indifferent crowd, to what wasn't the nearest table, where he made the mistake of placing the glass on a one-degree slant toward the weight of Vince Mansur's forearm, afflicted with its muscular giantism that hardly precluded the swift and precise employment of reflex which caught the salesman's arm before he could escape.

Woops. Meet a local ruffian.

By now Stella and I had crept up on the scene like lepidopterists, and we watched the glass slide so slick and fast it seemed motorized, off the table and then to the floor beside Vince's legs so slowly now that it seemed it had yet to hit when Vince already had swung the salesman back onto the empty chair beside him and was exhorting him to stay and drink.

"No, I really have to—"

"Nonsense! Right girls?"

"Nonsense," I added from over the shoulders of the two girls still tittering just beyond Vince's reach. Stella was already under the table fumbling for the tumbler, which had yet to break.

"Bobby!" Vince greeted me, "how long have you been standing there?"

"Since about 1949, I—"

"Join us, meet the girls: Lois and these two…"

"Riva."

"Marl."

"Right, Marl," Vince repeated, floating a 5-dollar bill at her. "Marl, I want you to run up to the bar and get five or six beers—as many as you can carry..."

Stella had been tugging at my pants, beckoning me. I squeezed between Vince and his captive co-ed, Lois, and got down there with Stella to help her marvel at Lois' legs, which were working like pistons, with the glass caught spinning between her feet. Stella was on her hands and knees like a terrier, transfixed by the weird splendor of the phenomenon, a child agawk at a 5-cent circus trick.

"And look at *this* guy," she said, indicating the lower half of the salesman, on the other side of Vince.

I was wedged in good, facing the wrong way, my lower spine pressing back into a metal table leg that responded with a subtle force transmitted in throbs by my head to the underside of the table, which Vince habitually pounded, reversing temporarily at the expense of my nervous complex the flow of pressure. I felt a great need to distinguish myself from that which was not animate. I was able to swivel my head by grinding it against the table. The right leg of the salesman was perfectly still; the left was agitating like a jackhammer; and between the two both hands were plucking at the houndsteeth of his crotch.

Meanwhile, Vince's left knee was slowly sealing off my exit, moving toward Lois' gams with the stealth of a panther approaching a crippled monkey.

Stella and I seemed to exist in our own pocket of sound.

"Look," I said, "let's just get the glass and get the hell out of here while we still can," simultaneously admiring the little vixen for being the kind of girl who would at the drop of a glass root easily under a table on a dirty tavern floor.

"We can't just take it from her, though," she reasoned. "We have to wait for her to release it."

Her logic struck me as a lifeline of precision in the turbulence of an infinite space, and as such I pulled back to examine the scene in its timeless aspect, that is to say, I took into account the persistent suspicion of simultaneity, relegating Stella and me, Stella on her hands and knees, a mop, a terrier, polishing the indefatigable grime of the tavern floor with the wool of her skirt, the sleeves of her batwing sweater, and me, wedged under there with her like a gargoyle bought by a nouveau riche savant and crowded into storage with a host of plaster imitations, relegating Stella and me to figures beneath a tavern table, a tavern table in a tavern, a tavern in a town, a town overflown by a bird, a crow, say, no, a peacock that looks down on this tavern and this town, and, say, the pimply split moon-white ass of John Hopkins studded hirsute and working like an oil pump, without optimism, and, say, on the southern flanget of this orbit, nearby, the richest card game in town, and down there, behind Totton's Hotel a regrouping of sailors sharpening their knives, Joe Kneifl wandering somewhere downtown or driving around disabusing his nostalgia, and there—see there in the window the bored omniscience of Maggie's eyes…

So under the table we stayed, Vince handing down two of the bottles Mavis or Rita brought back from the bar, peering through the forest of legs trying to guess which ones belonged to Buzzy, who it turned out never strayed from the side of Judge Swiggum, and never released Sissie Turner, whose loyalty was fortified by the free flow of Old Style beer, which is pure brewed and double brewed, a process called krausening, beers intended for me that made ever more adroit Buzzy's one-armed passes, and between us couples dancing, tables being restored to their upright positions when necessary, sedentary multipedes grinding cigarettes into the floor, punctuated by the repeated desperate moments when I had to dispatch the more agile Stella for the tumbler that kept flying from its centripetal mission, for instance its leap from the foot grasp upon the descension of the gorilla paw of Vince Mansur's onto Lois' thigh, the glass then donkey kicked by the salesman into the rubberlegged maelstrom, a veritable tumbler catastrophe, this time the tumbler really gone too far yet there being nothing for it but for the more mobile in our foxhole to assay out there to retrieve it come what may—and here I have to put some of this together from word of mouth—she crawled out just about the same time there appeared in the bar a sailor with a nose taped back to the rough center of his face, returned with a dozen or so cronies, looking for Joe Turner, a couple of them already wielding pool cues, and when I figured out what was happening I saw how inextricably Stella was on all fours in the middle of it, in fact between the swabbies and Joe, who was slow dancing with an admirer to "Kawliga," that Hank Williams song that's always ruined by the dozens of shitbirds Indian pounding the tables, an effect here that was like tribal drums inciting the battle, providing a fairly ominous atmosphere for the impending mayhem that Buzzy—Buzzy, of all people—interdicted heroically just as the broken-faced sailor was reaching for Joe's impervious, romantically inclined shoulder, which spun around and stopped at the crash of a bottle Buzzy brandished directly up to the neck of the aggressor, and held there, saying, "Go ahead and move," which he decided against long enough I was able to reach Stella and pull her out of the crowd of angry men closing in on the sailors, who just that quickly were ripe for realizing that they had collectively had a very bad idea.

One-Arm Buzzy

Wouldn't you know it would have to happen the night of the one heroic act of my life. Still, Sissie gave me a pretty good ride for it, a pretty good ride.

Bobby, Spring, 1954

If some genius ever figures out how to spot a bad luck streak before it starts I hope he meets up with the genius who figures out how to prevent it. The streak had already started when I spotted the cop light behind the bar at the Coo Coo Club. As soon as I saw it, I piped up.

"Since when did the Coo Coo Club mount a cop light behind the bar?"

Nobody heard me.

The siren was announcing tomorrow's hangover. I never understood why the siren was inside the light, and that seemed a good enough conundrum to mull over until someone—he was behind the bar, so I considered the possibility he might be a bartender—finally shut the goddamn thing off. He was young, healthy, handsome, eager, and nauseating me with his irreconcilable presence.

"Who the fuck hired you?" I asked, and suddenly a fat lady bore into my left periphery, squelching it like a boulder falling on a mushroom.

"Nobody," the guy said, and I somehow got the notion he might go by the moniker Dudley.

"Oh," I said with forced cheer, "you just went back there to shut off the light. Of course. Good lad."

"What? I'm bartending."

Now I pegged Dudley for a liar.

"Well what are you then, a *rogue* bartender?"

I could hear the fat lady breathing.

"What's that?" Dudley asked.

"A preposter, an intender, *not* the real thing."

"I don't know what you mean," Dudley said.

I turned to the fat lady.

"He doesn't know what I mean."

"Neither do I." She said. She held a tall glass full of pink fluid in both her hands.

"What's that," I asked, "Pepto Bismal?"

"It's Jeff's special birthday drink. Didn't you hear the siren?"

"Of course, I heard the siren, I can still hear the siren. Who's Jeff?"

"Him," she said, daring to hold the glass in one hand so she could point at Dudley with the other.

"The imposter?"

"What do you mean?"

I looked past her.

"Anybody in here know what I mean?"

But there was no one else in the bar.

"Somebody changed the place around."

"I did," Dudley said.

"Well, when Ernest finds out he ain't going to like it."

"Who's Ernest?" Dudley asked.

"When Ernest finds out, you're history—gone..."

The fat lady pinched my tricep.

"Who's Ernest?"

"Don't be coy with me, pinniped lady—and release my arm. I was in the Navy."

"Sorry," she said, returning her flipper to the birthday glass. "He's bound to turn up any minute."

"Who?" they asked in near unison.

"See if you can't guess—Ernest. Now give me another drink."

"Same?"

"Yeah—nothing pink."

Dudley went off to fetch the bourbon.

"I don't like this jerk," I confided to the fat lady.

"Jeff, he's—"

"No. Dudley."

"Who?"

"This guy." I pointed at Dudley, who was frowning at me, pouring my drink.

"Did you call me a jerk?" he asked.

"See what I mean?"

"No, I—"

I leaned in close and whispered into her ear, "I think Dudley killed Evelyn Hartley."

I don't know why that popped into my mind just then, except it was two days before that Stella had her little episode in the cement desert.

"Ah, Dudley, you're back."

"Did you call me a jerk?", he asked, somewhat repetitiously, making a show of withholding my drink.

"I'm not answering until you put the glass down."

"I'm not serving you until we straighten this out."

"You serve me or you'll answer to Ernest. Nobody cuts me off at the Coo Coo Club."

Dudley smarmed out a laugh that made me want to steam him on the spot, while the diva took to backhanding my arm, the same one as before.

"Hey," she said, "hey fella, this ain't the Coo Coo Club."

"The hell it ain't."

"No—it's his place. He *owns* it."

I thought the weight she leant *owns* would break through the crust of the earth, taking all the other words with it. Then I remembered her.

Dudley was still holding my drink out of reach and sporting a superior grin. I decided it was time to show him who he was dealing with. I lurched forward and made a wild swipe at the glass, which he jerked out of reach—a young, athletic man, he had superior reflexes—flibbing the bourbon and ice into the bottles behind.

Touché! Now it was my turn to laugh and Dudley was out of sorts.

"All right—that's enough—hit the pavement."

"Hit the pavement. That's good, but I'm not leaving until I get my drink—unless Ernest tells me to. Him I'll listen to. And he would never kick me out. And another thing, even when I do get my drink I'm not leaving because that would be stupid, walking out of here with a glass of bourbon in my hand. You think I'm stupid? You think you just hand over a glass of bourbon and a guy hits the pavement? Oh no, Prince Dudley, I'll take my bourbon sitting down. Now go get it or I'll tell more than just the birthday dame here who killed Evelyn Hartley."

"You're out of line, fella," he said, adding "way out of line" like that athletic type I fancied he might be, the one with the remorseless eyes, the amoral Nazi type who wouldn't stop kicking a fella once he'd hit the pavement, the kind who might fly over the bar in a bound and stomp out of me a regular turd without in the least disturbing the rarefied adolescence of his features. He might be one of these hateful morons born with a lucky star wedged in his rectum who could beat me at anything, including fisticuffs, which I was far too drunk to consider anyway.

"Why does everybody in this joint call me fella suddenly?"

"You leaving or do I make you leave?"

"Oh, let him stay, Jeff," the fat lady interceded on my behalf. "I don't have anyone to have my birthday drink."

Dudley's new look was thick with tolerance.

"With."

"What?" he asked.

"Nothing. Get me a bourbon. We'll start over."

"All right. Just to show I'm not a jerk."

I turned again to the fat lady.

"So what's the deal here, Ada? You say I'm not at present present at the Coo Coo Club?"

Of course, by now I was sober enough to know a terrible detour had been arranged for my evening.

"No, this is Jeff's bar."

"What's he call it?"

"*The Station House.*"

"Cop motif. Siren. I got it."

She leaned closer to show me someone's buttocks ampling out of the top of her birthday dress. Birthday boy.

"What's your name?"

"That's 50 cents," Dudley declaimed, with a certain veiled aggression that was in keeping with this strange new tavern world.

"Call it a birthday drink."

"I call it fifty cents."

The veil had slipped off the aggression.

"That's a lot of coin for a birthday drink. Isn't it her birthday?"

"It's my birthday, Jeff."

"So what. He's paying for the drink."

I knocked back half the bourbon and looked from Dudley to Ada.

"You know what I think, Ada? I think this really is the Coo Coo Club and I think Dudley here killed Evelyn Hartley and that's why they took his badge. I think he killed the girl, brought her here, and changed the place around so no one could find her anymore. And I'll be damned if I'm going to buy a drink off a murderer."

When I reached for my glass again, Dudley grabbed my wrist and squeezed like a zygodactyl trying to crack a macadamia nut.

"Get the money out of your pocket," Dudley said. My wrist certainly wasn't going anywhere.

"I can't—I need this hand. My money's on this side."

"Ada, get the money from his pocket."

"My names' not Ada."

"Dar—get the money—"

"Oh no—she's not fishing around in my pants, not the birthday girl. You made your point—let me go and I'll pay for the goddamn drink."

He leaned close to me without letting go.

"And then leave," he said, with too deliberate a menace for me to take seriously.

"Get your face away from me. Yes, and then leave."

"All right," he said, prematurely smug.

I put my hand in my pocket—the wrist felt like it was hand-cuffed.

"Wait," I realized, "I should get to finish the drink, then. I mean you can't hardly charge me for a drink and then refuse to let me drink it."

"He's right," Ada confirmed, still harboring faint birthday hopes. "What he's saying makes a lot of sense. He's only drank half the drink."

"Fine," Dudley decided. "I'll give you twenty seconds to finish your drink."

"That's fair," I told Ada.

"A time limit is fair," I told Dudley.

"Why don't you promise to behave and you can stay," Ada said as I plucked the ice cubes from my glass.

"Like I said, Ada," I said, placing the ice cubes on the bar where they sashayed into a tin ashtray, "I don't buy drinks from murderers," and I tossed the bourbon into Dudley's face, which next thing I knew was *behind* me—he had vaulted the bar and gotten my arm where no contortionist could have, and was running me toward the door we agreed would best be opened by my face, releasing me to my own momentum, which sprawled me to the curb and up against a brand new Packard.

I didn't like brand new Packards and I was afraid Dudley would collect himself and realize I still hadn't paid for my drink, so I crawled along the curb until I came upon an old

Plymouth with a running board, where I sat looking up at the neon windmill that alerted me to the fact that I was on Third Street outside the Melody Mill.

It was good to know where I was again. The windmill was blue and it was moving and it told me where I was. Or, looking again, someone was trying to make me think the windmill was moving. Or just the line of lights was blue. Or the lights were blue and not in a line but arranged to suggest the blades of a windmill, which was moving. Or two or three blade patterns lit up one after another to give me the illusion that it was moving. No, it was moving. It was revolving. And then it wasn't—two or three blade patterns were flashing alternately. Then it was revolving again and I wanted to vomit—but then the blade patterns were flashing alternately and I didn't have to vomit, unless I looked away, which I had to because the blades were revolving. But when I looked away the blades sped up so I looked back and caught them at rest, taking turns flashing, which they did until slowly, very slowly, the blades began to move again, luring me into its belief system so that I had to concentrate my gaze on the eye of the windmill to keep from vomiting, at which point they stopped revolving but continued to flash.

One of the blue lights turned green, and then the rest did, one by one at first, then suddenly all of them, except one, a peacock that flew away from the flock and disappeared like a comet. I no longer had to vomit—I was in the sky again, looking down at myself hunched on the running board of the Plymouth, a sad inebriate epiphenomenal self I could escape. As I flew—fast and effortless, I could always see myself down there on Third Street, invisible to passersby, my head in my hands, spreading my fingers to sneak a look at the windmill, at the peacock up in the sky—I could see the drunk on the running board, I could see the river a few blocks away and the islands and sloughs and bottoms, the West channel, the abrupt bend in the main channel, a few lights marking La Crescent, the little town in the break of the Minnesota bluffs, and to the east I could see where the houses besieged the bean fields— there's Viggo's house—and forests climbing the bluffs and atop the bluffs for miles farmland marbled by dark creases in the land, sudden valleys untillable, farmhouse outposts hiding anachronisms scratching the land into a new wilderness in a manner consoling for its isolation, bent figures folding sorrows away into the land, plump figures pacing by kitchen windows in expiring light, roads with no traffic...and to the north and south I could see how everything turned to the river in the end: I could see civilization radiating out from me and close by I could see where what we made empties into nothing, but I recognized no one, no one but me...somewhere out there was Buzzy, and somewhere Stella...a few cars plied the streets in slow geometries, shortly coming to rest, hiding like children by closing their eyes, and I closed my eyes yet still saw a lone man drunkhunched on a running board of a Plymouth, a peacock in the sky surveying the civilization built around me without connecting to me, no wires issued from me, no pneumatic tube umbilicalled me, me: devoid of meaning, a brown evanescence, my logic interred in an unmarked grave like Evelyn Hartley, my mystery alive and alert as Evelyn herself, and that goddamn windmill looking down on me, displaying its fraudulence over my head, and I was on my feet screaming before I knew I was on my feet screaming: "Stella!...Stella!...Stella!...", walking down the street screaming for Stella, ignoring the glutinous eyes of half-curious noctambulos, fleening me from habit, clutching each other lest one of them join me off that deep end..."Stella!", I cried, a cry familiar enough for contagion, and sure enough someone behind me—Dudley? Mocking Dudley?—shouted "Stella!", and I wasn't about to let up until I found her so I screamed "Stella!", oblivious to mockery I screamed "Stella!", and by now I'd reached Third and Pearl, that great intersection of tavern traffic, and behind me Dudley mocked: "Stella!", and a pack of women like jackals coming up Pearl decided to make it a procession, one of them crying "Stella!" and laughing and two or three others screamed it and before I was across the street Ada the fat lady was screaming "Stella!" behind me, and by the time I was halfway to Jay Street I could hear "Stella!"s going back a block behind me, dozens of them, and by the time Ada and I reached the Coo Coo Club, at least a dozen people were outside its doors crying "Stella!" and I must have been loud enough to drown out the juke box because Buzzy opened the door and walked out followed by Stella, who walked up to me and said, "What do you want," and the crowd broke into cheers and I hugged her like she was back from the dead.

One-Arm Buzzy

This used to be a hell of a place back when they had the trains coming through. My folks were train folks—and somehow to some nitwits that explains why I only have one arm, like as if I'd lost it on the tracks. The trains are gone now and probably for good, but there's still a lively corner there at Second and Pearl, what with Totton's Hotel and Tommy's Little Dandy, the Gannet Hotel and The Spot, and they'll still have whores there when I'm dead, they've always had whores on that corner and they always will. Until the night Bobby got lost and thrown out of the Station House my favorite was the Jap girl. She'd been there forever and never looked a day older since the war. She always wore those Chinese silk pajamas with the slit up the side all the way to her kidneys. I always wanted to talk to her, I always wanted to find out what she thought about things. What did she think of us blowing up their cities? Did she have family left after the war? I didn't even know if she was from Tokyo, or what. But she never spoke a word of real English, just baby talk like "You good, only need one arm…You my man…You come you ask for me…" Nonsense talk. And if I tried too hard, if I asked too many questions she would point out the time, as if to remind me that this equation was as lopsided as the rest.

I wouldn't say that the only time I go to Tommy's Little Dandy is to have a whore, but I would say that if I stay a while that's usually the way it ends up. I get to looking the Jap over, and watch her dance a couple times, and I suppose that's just exactly the way it's supposed to happen. But that night I was feeling pretty good for no particular reason, and I was smerving down one after another, and Tommy Tooke, the proprietor, was drunk as always, and picking like a fiend on his banjer, and I was having a hell of a time, and not thinking about anything in particular, maybe in a sort of daze, when suddenly the place seemed far too quiet to me. I guess Tommy had laid his banjer down. And it was a Monday night, so it's no surprise it wasn't all that crowded in there, and I sort of drifted my eyes around, sort of half looking for the Jap, not that I couldn't have come up with something else if she was busy, so I didn't care much I didn't see her. So naturally I got to piss, but through some sort of accident of disorientation I went for the bathrooms in the Coo Coo Club, which mistake made in Tommy's actually led you to a corridor that gets you into the Totton Hotel if the door's open, which it shouldn't be but was. And once in the corridor I realized my mistake but stumbled along with my momentum to that door which should never be left open, and right away I heard the Jap. Off to the right there's the employee lounge off the counter area of the Totton and she was in there with Tommy, and I knew it was her despite she was talking as good English as me, without an accent at all, and she was arguing with Tommy, and the way sound works you can tell when two people's in a clinch, a love clinch. So that's the way it was with them, and that's okay with me, but except for it was me they were talking about, and since that time I've learned a thing or two about the Japs so I guess it's a product of her culture that she cannot abide deformity. Yet at that moment her disgust came as a painful shock, the way she spat the word *cripple*, the way she pleaded…

I got the hell out of there never to come back, and the natural thing to do would have been to head straight to the Coo Coo Club, but those two blocks or so seemed awful far at the time, so I crossed the street over to The Spot, and there was no one in there but the Powder Puff Kid, as usual his face powdered like a goddamn Jap fan dancer, and I blurted out give me a five finger whiskey right away, and before I could stop him he's got it on the fucking Lionel train, heading away from me. I made a dash for it, shook enough I lunged with the wrong arm, the one not there, and before I could get my balance and reach with the other arm the train had made the turn at the back wall and there went my whiskey disappeared through the goddamn tunnel bridge, and then on the curve around the back of the bar headed for the mountains, through the long Alpine tunnel and out, all the way past the farmland and weaving through the city of bottles, and then the long slow turn again, and chugging up to the second shelf, where it whistles and he's got that crossing that works with the lights and the guards and everything, and a car with a little rubber family sitting in it, the perfect little rubber American family sitting there watching my giant whiskey go by—and I look over at the Powder Puff Kid and he's smiling at it like it's the first time he ever seen the goddamn thing, him and that goddamn rubber family watching my drink, which is now up on the third level where it rounds Pike's Peak, choo choos again so as to let me know how goddamn far I am from having my goddamn drink, and it takes just as long to get down from there, so I had time to calculate I'd get over to the Coo Coo and order and receive and drink my drink before the goddamn Lionel would return with my drink, so I said, "Pour it back in the bottle, Kid," and found Stella at the Coo Coo bar wondering where she'd left her man.

Gerard

They had one bar, the Underground, that had the booze in the basement and you went to the bar and wrote down your order and the messenger sent it by pneumatic tube to the bartender, who made the drinks and sent them back by pneumatic tube.

The problem with the place is they never figured out how to keep the drinks from spilling. It was a popular place for a few weeks before the novelty wore off and people started going where they could just go up to a man, ask for a drink, watch him make it, and then give it to you.

Todd Mills

"It's getting late."

Again, Adele merely smiled at me. And this time I finally had it figured out. Whatever you thought the smile meant, you were wrong. If you didn't think it was seductive, you weren't much of a man. If you thought it was seductive, you were being mocked.

She smiled, and she lit a cigarette. So it was not yet time for me to go.

Like all the stories this was not a story, and still it was not time to go.

The sun was gone, slipped quietly from the window and behind clouds. The scumble of yellow from the bulb behind me was not enough to cast my shadow to Adele.

Her smile was the smile of a girl Evelyn's age, but the smile was gone and her thought was in the smoke of her cigarette. Subcutaneous green pools pushed at the flesh under her eyes, and her lips looked pale and dry. And as I sat there letting her age in the crypt of my eyes, an imperceptible shift in the density of the air in the room suggested a part of her was aware of my observations, of my interest.

Her crossed leg rose and descended again, a further slope of thigh visible like a slattern's simple revelation, a mockery, an entrapment.

Still she gazed into her smoke.

The leg adjusted itself again and more was revealed and still she gazed into the smoke.

When I could no longer prevent myself from swallowing the saliva pooling in my mouth, the sound made was louder than the words we exchanged. Maybe that's what made her smile again, look young again, look me in the eyes again, and adjust her leg yet again.

Stubbing her cigarette out, she faced me with lustrous eyes and said, "You'll want to see the cellar before you go."

Bobby in Love

Stella Stella Stella Stella Stella Stella Stella Stevelyn Shmevelyn—bad dream, just a dream, here lies Stella. Here lies Stella's wrist. And here's the pulse. Bad dream, and priapic as a Romanian king: Down, dark side! A necrophilist's afterdream, what does it mean? This apperceptual witnessing of a sick moment, the afterdream and its cock sustained be velleity, the gradations of realization like the sliding shadow of a crude timepiece, mind

confronts instinct, the lush stillness of the scene and the nar-
cissistic love of one's own repulsion. Oh Stella, Stella, Stella...

Marla Rothgert

The dream is a bean in a pod, the dream is the bean splitting
open the pod. Rasputin is inside the dacha! Rasputin is inside
the dacha!

Bobby, Spring, 1954

I thought I'd never get another drink, and the thought of life
without bourbon, of course, made me fear eternity, and that
led me to playing tricks of disembodiment on myself, trying
to fool myself sober so to speak, which if I understood Stella
and Buzzy aright, was where I had to be before they'd let me
start getting drunk again, a methodological fallacy I hadn't
the means to vallarize vocally on the downslope of drunk to
sober, though I took the whole thing calmly as the ostensible
reason was so as to prevent my wandering off and confusing
one particular tavern with another. So I tried to remove myself
from the predicament by ruthlessly leaving myself behind,
a surprisingly simple task—if you're me—though I found it
necessary to cheat dramatically, overdoing same to the point
I sort of lapped myself and there I was following my ghost as
two hours earlier in the night it dashed out of the Coo Coo
Club in search of Buzzy, methodically searching bar to bar, and

only succumbing to surfeit of drink after the fifth tavern (or so, of course—or so!) (goddamnit, I said or so), the sixth of which was that new one, the Station House, where I figured I shouldn't be, so I went off again for the Coo Coo Club where it all started.

What happened was Ed Black, my man on the force, a decent copper, a lug, a kind-hearted son of a bitch, a credit to his badge, burst into the Coo Coo Club looking for his better bosom pal Buzzy, who wasn't there.

It was around 11 p.m., and while Stella and I sat at the bar pretending I was 15 and she was 30, entire universes had been convulsing over at the Hopkins house, where events had forever proved their independence by occluding every avenue both toward and from deception. The deception had cut off its own escape route. The Hopkins husband found out everything. The cuckold cucracked, went cuckoo. By 11 o'clock he knew everything and if it would've been impossible to know the name of every man who ever fucked his wife, he at least had memorized the repeat offenders, most one-armed of which was our very own Buzzy.

When Ed ran into the bar, Hopkins was running loose with a shotgun.

Carrying on a theme of the night, I sent half myself into a panic and the other half wondering how soon Hopkins would realize he was better off an orange-haired, ruddy-faced, oblivious simpleton than an enraged cuckold aloose in the city hunting down an impossible number of his wife's paramours. He'd be lucky to get even one of them, I figured. Yet if he figured that way, that one would be the easiest to pick off, the easiest to find, to wit Buzzy. Hence the paradox. Hopkins simply wasn't the type of man who would know how properly to avenge his decimated honor, which is probably why an uncanny number of people who liked him well enough could not bring themselves to tell him what his wife was doing behind his back/on hers every night he went to work. Weirdly, then, the danger to Buzzy was real for the very reasons it should not have been.

"Plus," Buzzy said later, as I drank my ice water, "most of us who knew were guilty, or planning to be someday."

Stella shot me a look.

"Is that all you can think about at a time like this?"

"Well," she asked, "did you?"

"Not since we got together."

"How many times?"

I ignored her.

"But that still only covers about half—not counting women. No, nobody told him because by some freak of nature—and you know I'm no phrenologist—by some freak of nature he was born a cuckold. To tell him would've been like kidnapping an eskimo and turning him loose in New York City with five bucks in his wallet."

"What?"

"How many times?"

"Nine and a half."

"You're disgusting—she's a cow."

Buzzy wasn't about to take that.

"I could have lost my life over that woman," he said. "Maggie Hopkins is an okay woman. And she's been through a lot—"

"And a lot have been through her."

"—and she's about to go through a great deal more."

"Besides," I added, "as a mammal she cannot help sending out her call, her scent, her musk, as it were. Men have to answer that call. You think I'm sober enough, yet? I'm sounding pretty smart."

It was Harmon Schnellinger who answered the call this particular night. A short, genial house painter, Harmon had once knocked Vince Mansur out cold with a short right cross after tiring of Vince's trying to bully him off a girl he was dancing with at the Avalon. Harmon was always the guy who didn't have a date, and usually didn't seem to care. You got to assuming he didn't really need to have sex, that he was a neutral, which was probably why Vince felt free to jack his woman, and more to the point why it was ironic Harmon was balling old lady Hopkins the night she got caught.

Imagine John's surprise. Now imagine it again.

John left on schedule at 10:15 and Harmon pulled up at 10:16. Let's just say I'm close enough. Maggie and him must have hit the sack right away. Judge Hamilton Swiggum, who'd been drinking up the street at the Jungle, got in his car, parked at the end of the block Hopkins lives on, which was parked with both wheels on the right side up on the curb. He must've figured in that drunken streamline way that if he kept going straight eventually the tires would have to fall back to the street, probably at the end of a block—and the faster he went the sooner it would happen, so he was moving pretty good when he hit the hackberry tree in the Hopkins boulevard. A patrol cop saw the whole thing and was on Swiggum in seconds, before he knew who he was dealing with. The judge was unhurt. He remained in the car, sitting bolt upright as always, staring at the tree like it was the perpetrator of some minor and mystifying crime.

Here's where you have your proof of the contagion of bad luck: roughly a mile away, on South Avenue, John Hopkins gets pulled over for speeding. He's all agitated, worrying over being late for work, the cop behind him is taking his time writing up the ticket, he can't sit there any longer, he leaps from the car to go back and ask the cop to hurry or he's going to be late for work, and right then the accident is called over the radio.

"717 Market! That's my house!"

And he's off. He runs back to his car, pulls a U-turn, screeches home.

"That's one thing I can't figure," Buzzy said. "Why'd he have to rush home? Over a goddamn tree?"

"He didn't know it was a tree, I think."

"He's so worried about being late for work, which he never is—I'd never hire a guy like that, it ain't human—and yet he rushes home because of a tree…"

"That's not it," Stella said. "He probably just heard the word accident, or ambulance, and then the address."

"No," Buzzy insisted. "I got this from Eddie. The call over the radio said they had Swiggum there, ran into a tree at 717 Market. I mean I was adamant on the point: Why'd he have to rush home? Here's exactly what the radio said—I rememorized it: 'We got Swiggum here, run into a hackberry tree, 717 Market.' So why'd he rush home?"

"Maybe he had an inkling," Stella suggested.

"What I'd like to know is why Harmon was still there when Hopkins got home. A goddamn car crashed into a tree in the yard and he just kept on plowing?"

"Maybe they didn't hear it," Buzzy figured.

"No," Stella objected. "They're having sexual intercourse, they just got started, a car hits a tree they say so what. What's it got to do with them? Why would they worry about Hopkins coming home."

"They could have at least checked to see if anyone got hurt."

"Maybe they did, Buzz," I said. "They get up, or better she does, she goes to the window, looks out, calls back 'Nothing, dear, it's just Judge Swiggum plowed into our tree,' and she goes back to bed. Enter Johnny."

Hopkins arrived home ahead of all the official vehicles, but not before Judge Swiggum had bucked his car a couple times before finding reverse and backing away from the tree, lurching to the street and away, followed by the copper, so that the scene was as he'd left it but for the bark stripped off the tree and the Schnellinger vehicle parked up ahead where it would have stopped the judge's car if the tree had not been there. Perhaps more importantly it would have made for a louder collision, one that would have more definitively interuptussed the couple entwined in that small grunting groping zone of oblivion that did not admit or was not disturbed by the sounds of cars hitting trees, keys turning locks, footsteps of husbands—the scene previously enacted several million times: the cuckold's premature return to the nest, he pauses in the doorway, she never sees him right away, but she always sees him first, before the man does—the shit has been flying at the fan but hasn't hit yet, and this interval, this pause, this is her moment of pure triumph, and she does not here formulate her response, which will be what it will be (what are you doing back here?; sit down, we'll be done in a moment; Johnny, I want you to meet somebody; I don't know Johnny, it just…happened; uh, rape?; wouldn't you know I get caught the first time; you like to watch? do ya?; where'd that other guy go?; {laughing} sorry; go ahead, kill me, I don't care anymore; etc., or *ad infinitum*) but only after she luxuriates in the absurdity both men are forced to labor through deprived of free will, the husband suddenly graduated from fool to fool who knows, the lover gone from lover to scrabbler in domestic still life—Maggie luxuriates as one stammers and the other grunts, uttering past each other while she floats a last second dreamlike, alone in a warm bed under a bovinity of blankets, the wind outside yowling and swirling, faster and faster, becoming the blades of the fan a split second before the shit hits.

"I still don't see how they didn't hear it," Buzzy said.

"Especially," I pointed out, my mind sharpened by the bourbon they finally let me order, "on a night like this when she would have the windows open."

"You'd know, wouldn't you?"

"Christ, Stella...what do you want me to say. That I was desperate, all right I feared impotence, I was desperate to know."

"Don't speak of her that way."

"Come off it Buzzy—she's not dead."

"My point," Buzzy insisted, "is it's a little uncomely of you two to be arguing over a matter of petty jealousy when you should be more concerned about Maggie's future. She's in a pretty rough spot now."

"Who put her there?"

My Stella knew hypocrisy when she saw it.

"What?"

"You screwed her once a week and you pretend to be concerned? What did you think would happen? The old man went off with a shotgun—he could just as easily have turned it on her. You had to know that in the back of your mind that something big was at risk so that little bone of yours could get its weekly scrubbing. You fuck a man's wife—"

"But, what I want to get at," I interrupted, seeing that Stella's accusation was having its effect on poor Buzzy, who was assuming the look of a teenager who had blinded his own dog with a bb gun, "is how they could possibly not have heard anything."

Stella looked at me like Jane Greer in no mood to apologize.

"You're usually not this naïve, Bobby."

Yet the mad husband Hopkins must not have had too much trouble interrupting the fracas, for the cop who was ticketing him and the rest of them were just minutes behind him and by that time Harmon was already gone, apparently having escaped while Hopkins, whose intuition burst into a cataract of implications—this couldn't be the first adultero flagrante and he just happened upon it—confronted his wife, a scene the ticketer cop unwisely shied away from, allowing Hopkins to slap a few names out of his wife and escape out the back door with the shotgun that endured from days prior to citification, Maggie running naked and hysterical out the front door shouting names prominent and otherwise to the milling, grass-toeing cops waiting for the interrogation to subside, one of whom was Ed Black, who heard Buzzy's name, not that he didn't already know, but now knew that John Hopkins knew, and so made straight for the Coo Coo Club, while the rest of the cops made out a comprehensive list.

One of them had the foresight to get on the radio and alert the entire force, including the officer who had Swiggum pulled over on Weston Street and wondered what to do with him and was told leave him the hell alone and get after the man with the shotgun, forget the whole thing happened, leave the judge roaming the streets with one headlight and drunk as a judge.

"It's lucky he didn't kill someone tonight."

"That's true every night."

"Why couldn't the cop have just taken his keys?"

Buzzy and I looked at each other.

"Take Judge Swiggum's keys," I chuckled, "get a load of the dame."

"What?"

"Tell her, Buzzy."

"You ever see anyone try to take Judge Swiggum's keys?" he asked rhetorical by way of starting.

He even waited for Stella to answer.

"No, tell me."

"I'll tell you why in case you don't know."

"I just said I don't know."

"Well, there's as they say in court, a president to this. A bartender and a couple patrons one night tried to take the judge's keys away from him. Right here at the CCC. I was here. This is maybe 10, 12 years ago. I don't remember the bartender's name, but one of the customers was Danny Stratton, a nice enough fella, though his wife is kind of a slug. They tried to restrain the judge, reach in his pocket for the keys. I never saw someone so outraged as the judge—like as if someone reached out and pinched Eleanor Roosevelt in the nipple. Very slowly, very deliberately, the judge—remember he's a big man and this is ten, maybe—"

"Twelve."

"—twelve, years ago. He knocked all three of them out, one by one, one punch each, grabbed them by the neck with one of them big hands and crushed them with a long slow punch like a hammer. Then he walked out of there and drove home and nobody's ever tried to take his keys off him since."

"Gee." Stella said, and even I could not distinguish her awe from her sardonicism.

"There's more. Years later—and I mean *years*, like there was a war in between, Stratton came before the judge on a divorce thing. He and his wife they had it all worked out, it was mutual and they agreed on everything. They called it cruelty, I guess, just because they had to call it something. The judge, though, he started grilling the old lady for instances, browbeating her so she got scared. He told her if she calls it cruelty and there's no cruelty she goes to jail for perjury, and so she testifies Danny beat her, and then he has Danny locked up, arrested on the spot for battery and assault. It took weeks for lawyers to straighten the whole thing out and get Danny out of jail because now *they* were scared shitless, too, because they saw that afternoon how it could all come down to Swiggum's law, and the books they know ain't worth a goddamn thing in his court. I talked to one of them once. You know Al Bettke? He was in on this. I said, 'Jeez, Al, didn't you know better? Danny'd never hit anybody.' And he says, 'You know, Buzz, I'd be thinking apropo the judge "he can't do this," and then that booming voice would lay down *his* law, and I'd want to object but when I tried to open my mouth I'd be thinking if I do he'll *ruin* me. Buzzy there's the law and there's the law, but there's no higher authority than what Judge Swiggum had in his voice that day. Danny Stratton tried to take his *keys*.'"

"He did get out of jail, though…", Stella wondered.

"Sure. Course he did—but nobody ever got a worse divorce settlement."

"Hopkins won't either."

"They'll blame it all on her?" Stella asked, genuinely concerned.

"The town slut—"

"Watch it!"

"I'm just saying what they'll say, Buzzy. I know there's plenty of other sluts in this town."

I don't know by what obtuse subconscious decision we both looked at Stella, but she chose to take the matter up with Buzzy.

"You don't get on a slut's good side by bringing it up."

Buzzy threw up his arm and his imaginary arm.

"I didn't say anything."

"Besides," Stella pressed on, "a slut is only a woman who acts like a man."

"That's about half right," I conceded, "but let's get on with the Hopkins saga."

What probably happened to Hopkins shortly after he ran out the back door like a commando is he was gripped by target hysteria: so many targets, such concentration of fury. It's not hard to kill somebody on a Saturday night—everybody's easy enough to find—Buzzy at the Coo Coo Club, Skumsrud at the Brewhouse card game, to name a prominent two...and for that matter, a couple shots in the Coo Coo Club with a scattergun would probably yield a dozen guilty parties. All Hopkins had to do was choose a victim. But which? Should he rush down looking for Buzzy? He'd find me, Vince, Vince's brother the Fruit From Beirut, Joe Turner, Tyrone, I don't know about Ernest...Or should he indeed go break up the poker game, go after the big shots (as well as Stella's own brother, Timmy Markle, about whom I hadn't the heart to tell her even with Hopkins running loose with a murderous heart), or ambush one of the cops—Maggie may have clammed up about cops, but surely Hopkins must have figured her for at least a few men in blue. Oh grand deception! His mind must have been chaos…oatmeal…He ended up on the Cass Street Bridge, but my guess is he took something other than a direct route, even if the cops did find him there a mere half hour after he went looking for his rampage. Running out the backdoor (shotgun hefted two-handed, across his body, gun parallel to the ground, like a soldier), Hopkins would be heading north, at full speed, knowing the cops were accumulating in his own front yard, would soon be alerted by his wife and be coming after him. He'd emerge on Ferry Street, feel overly exposed, dash between houses, at this point having some vague notion about the greatest concentration of targets being downtown whereas the poker game would require stealthy backtracking through a dragnet; yet no specific target in mind, he'd turn left, hug the garages in the alley between Ferry and Division, make the next mad dash—across Seventh—turn toward Division halfway down the next block, falling to his belly on the turf next to a hedgerow, gun before him, facing Division Street, where he sees…nothing. No cops, none of the men who've been fucking his wife. He's now three blocks from home, five and a half blocks from the bridge, though he still doesn't know that's where he's heading. His future is five and a half blocks long plus half the bridge, a confrontation with the police, then a jail cell—what he sees is an infinite labyrinth with corpses he drops at every turn. Where to start? The biggest hypocrite. The guy everybody loves. The last guy you'd think would fuck a guy's wife: One Arm Buzzy. One arm: easy to spot from a distance. Maybe he's still at his gas station. Hopkins leaps to his feet, flies the land route back to Ferry, where he realizes the cops will be swarming Market Street, where Buzzy's Skelly Station is. Besides, the station is closed Saturday Nights, Buzzy'll be drunk downtown. Maybe he even sees a prowl car as he's about to cross Ferry. He flattens himself against a house until the car passes, then slinks back to the alley, thinking he needs to get out of the residential neighborhood, needs to get down to Second Street. But he's got to be careful—and he tries to be, at first looking both ways before crossing the street (Sixth) before realizing, in a hazy sort of way, that he's a madman with a shotgun, a cuckold on a spree of mad vengeance, delirious from the blood he intends to spill. It's they who need to be careful— they, them, the cops, the adulterers, all or any abominations that get in his way, or come into his sight. It beats working! So it doesn't take him long to arrive at Second and Division—he runs right down the middle of the street like an infantryman chasing a retreating army...only suddenly the army has disappeared. At this point we know he doesn't have long to get to the middle of the bridge. He's made this strategic point from where he can slide up to the Brewhouse *or* downtown to the taverns. So one of two things must happen: a) Hopkins is overwhelmed by the task ahead; i.e., here the hysteria takes hold: too many men have fucked his wife, and he cannot kill them all; b) when he comes upon the bridge (having decided to head to the Coo Coo Club) he suddenly gets the idea to get on it so he can jump off it—the same conclusion scenario a) leads to: somebody's got to die—some kind of absolute is necessary; killing a fraction of those who violated the sanctity of his marriage is not an absolute; killing the one person so egregiously victimized *is* an absolute, ipso facto: suicide. Hopkins on the bridge, passing motorist spots him (man with shotgun), cops are called, half hour passed, stand-off on bridge.

"As stand-offs go, it wasn't much."

"No, not much."

"Pretty pathetic."

"Ed told me," Buzzy said, "he had no clear idea what he wanted."

"To get him to put the gun down."

"Right. He said Hopkins didn't even seem to realize the gun had anything to do with it."

"Any persuasive power."

"It took a while for everyone to realize that Hopkins didn't intend to use the gun, and it was the gun that was keeping the cops at bay."

"Even though he wasn't pointing it at them."

"Even though he wasn't pointing it at them. It was Ed who figured it out. He said, 'Can we have the gun, John?', and John looked down at the gun like he forgot he had it. He—"

"He just gave it to me, kind of said 'oh, here.' And I took him in my car."

"Ed."

"Hey Ed."

"He came along peaceably, as they say...And then I'm about to turn off the bridge and there's Buzzy come walking along, so I called out the window to follow me to the station—he wasn't going to believe this."

"So," I asked him, "where *were* you."

"I was at the station. I stopped there earlier for some cash and got to doing a few things, you know them air vents on the—"

"You *were* at the station? You could be dead now."

"I hadn't thought of that."

"Anyway," Stella cut in, and I didn't like the way she was looking up at Ed, imbuing her adulation with what I knew to be desire.

"Anyway," Ed continued, "John cracked up in the car on the way to the station—he confessed to the murder of Evelyn Hartley."

"Did he?"

"Does he have an alibi?"

But I figured there was no way a cop would hook up with a 15-year-old girl, at least not a straight arrow like Ed Black…

"Why would he offer an alibi if he were confessing?"

"Should be easy to check, anyway."

And then I thought trying to control a mind like Stella's would be like adopting one of the Bowery Boys. Better just to let her get it out of her system, which she soon managed in her own way.

"So Hopkins confessed to killing Evelyn Hartley?" Stella sought to confirm.

Ed now looked directly at her. I'd never thought him handsome before, but when he turned his brown eyes on Stella I saw him step suavely out of his cop context, through the lounge of a swank hotel, and on into the bar.

"He insisted on it," Ed said.

This seemed to incite/excite Stella even more—her ass made the short leap to the edge of her chair like a flaming lemming, bringing her face another foot or so closer to Ed's, which responded by leaning forward so they were closer still. Ed was stiff-arming the table so no one would get hurt.

"Where is she?" Stella asked.

The bar was closing.

It took Ed a good twenty seconds to respond and all he could come up with was, "What?"

I understood, and Stella looked at me and knew it.

"Didn't you ask where he put her body?"

"No, don't you see," Ed told her, unable to repress the condescension of the cop trained to render the obvious, "he didn't really kill her. He was in a state of distress. He would've said anything…"

"Bar time!" Ernest called, and he only did it once.

Stella and I stood and she said to me softly, taking my arm, "I can't believe he didn't ask where he dumped the body."

In the river, of course, is what Hopkins would have said.

Chorus, Girls

Call it a river baptism, a flow and return, call it a dive in my Mississippi—eye pee pee eye, yesyes, call it a dammed river, Evelyn mangled in the first dam downriver, call it eternal flow and return, a river slough between our thighs, where the water slows, a languid slough, yet always flow, face down in a stagnant pool, washed up on the shore of a poisoned lake, dredge the river she's not there, drag that bitch out by the hair, toss her there for the vultures, bloat her, split her, waterlogged, slipped off like a glove, bloated and pale, the blue of disease, the green of undersea, flow like the river, men that are babies like our hands on their heads down there, the rise and subside of oceans, tides, silver fish, rapids, deliver her mangled, standing water in the ditch, what's that over there?, gray blue split hump arisen twixt the lily pads, hold their heads down there, their heads down there, don't let them up, don't let them to come up for air.

Bobby, Oct. 24, 1953

The sailors weren't gone five minutes when Sissie dragged her hero Buzzy out the door; the salesman had fled in the ruckus; Mrs. Skumsrud had vaporized inside the tacit knowledge that she'd be reconstituted on her barstool a week or sooner hence; Ernest interred to any of the multivarious transmogrifections expectable, was passing his hand in front of Judge Swiggum's eyes, unable to elicit a response; Joe Turner, flanked by the college boys recently sharked by his brother, wore on his face the baleful look of a man too easily swayed by the regard of children, yet bored; for some reason his bimbo sat on her ass across the floor near where Stella and I had been—it could be she'd just given up looking for the same glass Stella had in her mitts and wasn't about to relinquish; Nick, sober as something besides a judge, dapper from a trip to the toilet, where he always counted his money—reasoning that if he was discrete enough some of his victims would set aside future donations—and wetcombed his black hair, before returning to sit quietly at the bar sipping ice water until closing time; Vince had chased the college girl to another table and now had his tongue down past her tonsils;

her friends watched from the bar with a mixture of entreaty and creeping oblivion; Stella held the glass she'd earned above her head and began to dance, twirling perilously close to the floor grate, her skirt carouselling above her knees as she twirled faster and faster, the whole time looking up through her empty chalice, finally finding her center in the middle of the grate—maybe her heel got fortuitously stuck; Tyrone looked at me and I shrugged and he pressed the button and Stella's skirt covered her eyes and she whirled faster, a whirligig in pink underwear, a top of spun delight; and the judge disembarked abruptly from his stool, following his monomania directly into the women's bathroom, where he couldn't have known a wooden phallus planted by the sink had an alarm rigged to it, the sound of which normally produced salvos of roguish laughter, fired toward the door of the toilet as if Emiliano Zapata were coming out, but in this case mortified the tavern to silence—even the jukebox inexplicably cut off mid-Prima—and a stillness absolute but for Stella's centrifugal declension (her dress had reestablished her modesty, Tyrone having quit with the button now that something potentially serious was afoot). The judge was in there long enough for the alarm to subside and everyone to cast eyes downward in a unity of trepidation that grew all the more acute when the honorable Swiggum emerged with the instrument in his hand, wires dangling like the tail of a Madagascarene primate. Speaking for no one else: in my own effort to stifle laughter I bit my forefinger hard enough to draw blood, at the same time the intensity of relief at not being Ernest quelled any suspicion that I might somehow be in trouble, which I imagine as roughly similar to what everyone in the bar but Ernest himself was undergoing, not to speak for them. So I didn't have to bite through the bone. Yet Ernest did not come out all that bad himself, for the judge merely approached him, planted the missile upright on the bar, watched it topple from the imbalance of the bunched wiring, and declared, "**I have broken this object, Ernest.**"

Ernest lolled his head as if the knowledge imparted by the judge made it too heavy, and muttered, "Naw, oh, naw, Judge, it was already loose, we were aiming to get it fixed. Naw, it was already broke…"

The judge's brows clicked into furrow and he said, "**I see. Then I am not to be held liable.**"

"You want a coffee?" Ernest eructed incongruously, but by then the judge had aboutfaced and was headed with the resolution of a bullet toward the door.

Stella tugged at my arm.

"It won't be Ernest this time, will it?"

"Huh?"

"I think Nick's going to say it."

"Oh…No, no—it'll be Tyrone."

"Double the bet?"

"No, let us not be carried away for it is the ritual that matters."

The judge was out the door, a jet trail of silence attenuating the moment he had embodied with his terrible and gracious majesty. Nothing had changed, not yet, nothing had changed but it waited, a ball bearing momentarily jarred loose, a nothing on the roll seeking the bottomless nest it will come to rest in, that it will find without intention, and will nullify with its giantism.

And as if the pause consumed even the consciousness of all who remained in the tavern, Tyrone suddenly said, "One of these days he's going to kill somebody," and I had won back the money I lost on the salesman.

La Crosse Tribune

October 26, 1953: Eau Claire Salesman Brought in for Questioning

October 29, 1953: Drifter Arrested: Hartley Connection

November 9, 1953: Professor Hartley Passes Exam

January 22, 1954: Madison Man Questioned in Hartley Case

January 23, 1954: Duluth Mechanic Queried in Hartley Case

March 2, 1954: Waukon Man Grilled in Hartley Case

March 2, 1954: Laborer Brought in for Questioning in Hartley Case

March 4, 1954: Cornell Man Ribbed in Hartley Case

March 5, 1954: St. Paul Man Held in Connection with Hartley Case

March 24, 1954: Oshkosh Man Welcomed for Questioning in Hartley Case

April 20, 1954: La Valle Man Tickled Over Hartley Case

June 28, 1954: Police Will Question Fairmont Man

June 30, 1954: Gopher Man Spanked in Hartley Case

August 30, 1954: Wausau Truck Driver Truncheoned in Hartley Case

October 21, 1954: Transient to be Quizzed in Hartley Case

May 21, 1956: Serviceman Collared, Released

Detective Les Sorenson, 1967

I think it was Tabbert of the highway police who let the cat out of the bag regarding the Robinsdale Peeper. The Robinsdale Addition was actually in Shelby, outside the actual city limits of La Crosse, so it wasn't our province. But we knew about it. We had known about it for a long time. If you look at a map you can see how close it is to the Rasmussen place, where the girl was taken. Police had been receiving reports for the past year, before Evelyn was taken, on a roughly weekly basis, of a window peeper in that area. Worse yet, it occurred practically every rainy night in summer. Now there's a lot of reasons you don't want something like this to get out. First off, you don't want to alert the criminal. Secondly, when a more serious crime takes place, you don't want this criminal to suspect that he's under suspicion. Thirdly, you don't want the public to start thinking you bungled the case in that you had known for a year about a dangerous man at large and had done—in the public perception—nothing about it. Incidentally, this was not my case, so I can't speak to how it was handled, but this much after the fact I think I can at least express my dismay over the highway patrol's inability to capture a window peeper who was reported at least, at least, fifty times in one year. It may or may not reflect on anyone's abilities or decisions regarding the allocation of resources. In the city, I think it's safe to say that no single sex offender commits more than a few flashings before we catch him, and window peepers have been even easier to nail. Now after some time, if the public still has not been notified in some way of these circumstances, once the information does come out, as it will inevitably—rumors will radiate from, in this case, the Robinsdale Addition, where people live with this knowledge and talk to each other about it—once this information comes out, there will be a scandal. I believe Tabbert released the information because rumor and innuendo forced his hand. It didn't look good. In one particular case the summer before Evelyn was taken there was a report of a man at a window, his leering face appeared at the *basement* window, and he laughed at a woman who was I recall ironing clothes at the time, and he told her he was going to "get" her.

A great number of reports were made after that incident, but none after the Evelyn event.

Bobby, Spring, 1954

The laugh on the face of Satan is never without complicity, and he knows that, and is very patient with us. What he cannot stand is the meek and holy averting of the eyes. He's lonely, and he likes attention.

I hadn't seen Steve privately since the week after Evelyn was removed from the board. But I was curious since he'd gone underground, across with Charon after the Slade wench pitched him. He was an impressive transmogrifixer. In just one week his facial hair had tapered to a red goatee and the curls of his unwashed head hair formed two rudimentary horns, and his eyes were just beginning to take on the fanatic open intensity of absolutism.

The eyes suggested the beard and horns were not a costume and I therefore could not help but laugh.

I found him in a small brick house on the 800 block of Johnson, six blocks west from the Hartley manse, the kind of house—set a few feet back from the neighboring houses less than 30 inches away on either side—that's always dark, always has the shade drawn over the one small window facing the street, that's the first place you'd look for an urban hermit. You half expect a rotten smell within. But I'm sure he didn't intend to fool anybody—eyes like his are trained on the far end of the dark vortex within.

He waited for me to stop laughing before inviting me into his monastic living room. The room was about 8 by 10, with one doorway leading to the kitchen and the other to a bedroom. There was nothing on the walls but their evergreen paint, and only two wood chairs for furniture. Overhead a hatch presumably led to the attic where he was tossed out by God.

"Should I make myself comfortable," I asked, taking a seat.

Steve pulled the other chair over to face mine and sat down so close our knees were almost touching.

"How've you been? How's Stella?"

His voice was incongruously eager, not like the voice of the devil at all.

"Fine, everybody's fine. We're on a sort of bad slide, but fine. Seen another human since last Saturday?"

"I see people all the time. I get groceries."

"Other than that?" I looked around the bare room. "No phone? No newspapers, no radio. You don't even see your family, do you?"

"Did they send you here?"

"Of course not. You don't see them."

"I'm sure they'd rather not."

"They still put money in your bank account and leave you alone."

"In that regard they're enlightened."

"Good, good."

I had no idea whether the ensuing silence was awkward or not. After a minute or two Steve left the room and returned just as the splenetic sound of a violin at too high a speed broke down on me from both sides. I located the two metallic apertures that looked like infundibula pounded high into the front and back walls.

"You got it on the wrong speed, pal."

"No, it's a Paganini piece."

"That explains it."

"Yes, it does, doesn't it," he confirmed without irony.

We listened for a while until the next, slower tune delivered its exegesis on a different aspect of madness.

"He played, too, but of course this isn't him...though it might be. He was so good, and his own pieces so powerful and intricate and difficult to perform, he had no trouble convincing people he had made a pact with the devil. I believe he probably did."

After hearing a few tunes, I was inclined to agree. The fifth caprice sounded like mice running up and down a wire.

"Can't you just ask?"

"What is that supposed to mean?" he replied with an ingenuous inflection and an inscrutable smile.

"Nothing."

We listened to the violin stalling fortuitously and inevitable into a stasis of despair, the madness breaking into a clarity of utter anguish.

"So are you just dropping by, or did you have a reason?"

"I had a reason—gossip. But I'm still trying to read your mood."

"And you can't."

"No."

"A step in the right direction."

"What's that mean?"

He smiled.

"My mother did visit me once. I drove her right out of here with my Paganini—"

"If I'll pardon your incestuous turn of phrase."

"Yes. As soon as I put it on she was like a hell hound recoiling from a douse of holy water."

"Only it's the reverse."

"Right. She literally could not stand it. Isn't that interesting? As if a pure soul too weak to stand contact with evil. A moment of religious conflict. The devil chased her out, and he had himself a good laugh in doing so. I watched her outside—she crossed herself."

Paganini. Once in a while there would be a few lovely notes, snatched from some conventional melody, and immediately a lower chord would set about mocking them. It made me think of a man I knew in the Navy who wrote me about being duped by a transvestite in Manila after the war. That kind of thing can change a man. In fact, I wrote back but never heard from him again.

"So do you want to hear about Veronica or not?"

"I know about Veronica."

"The word catfight do anything for you?"

"I like the word catfight."

"Well, let me tell you, since I saw you last it's been a bad slide. Just after we left you at the Club, I ran into Vic Veglan and somehow started off on his bad side and ended up with a vague promise to a duel with knives. I think that particular climax comes tomorrow night at the Avalon. Stella's got me going to see Gene Vincent and the Blue Caps—"

"Children's music."

"Stella's 15."

"Touché...Not that I'm trying to be funny. But watch that shitbird—he's a tough bastard, and he's mean. He won't let it slide. And I'm not saying you don't know how to take care of yourself, but I don't think you'll see any scars on Veglan."

"He's not in the penitentiary either. I'll be swell. Back to the narrative. Monday night I get so drunk I get lost and wake up in the wrong bar only not so convinced it's the wrong bar. I get tossed out physically by a handsome SS officer. Same night Buzzy gets a raw deal from a whore. Two nights later Judge

Swiggum finally hits something—a tree—which would be just fine, nobody hurt, one headlight out, except he hits a tree with such specificity that it leads to John Hopkins finding out his old lady's been balling a major demographic swath of the town, so he runs loose with a shotgun, and he barely misses running into an oblivious Buzzy. He goes to jail, confesses to the murder of one Evelyn Hartley. He is not taken seriously. Bad omens are piling up. Hopkins shot no one. Swiggum killed no one. Buzzy still has an arm left. Stella still likes me. Then last night the catfight. You like the word, eh? Then let me tell you something. As I'm sure you know, I saw Miss Slade once and refused ever to look at her again, veritably Ulysseslike. Unlike you like. I hadn't your fortitude, nor the curiosity to attempt a foray into the eye—or anus, one might suspect—of that hurricane. Or take your volcano: I'm content to know they blow molten rock out their crania. No desire to get down in there, though I admit some interest in the whole Pompeiian phenomena, especially because you know it seems only by accident that it's not that way, that we freeze when we die. Can you imagine that…"

"Vast cemeteries of death beds…"

"No, think if it were required that we die while engaged in ordinary quotidian activity: me, crouched over a tire, on permanent display; you, spending your parent's money, reading Paracelsus—"

"How'd you know about that?"

"Informed guess. Paracelsus, Plotinus, Scluvius the Potter, Saint—"

"Who? Who was that third one?"

"I made that one up."

"Shitbird. So what about the catfight?"

"That I didn't make up. It was real and a good one. The best I've ever seen. Only one I've ever seen."

"What's it have to do with volcanos?"

"Everything. Veronica's ass is central, if split, and nothing if not a volcano. And her breasts—what are they if not volcanos...But before last night these were only suspicions of mine, not that I had any doubt, but or because I refused to look. I've even allowed her to drive me out of the Coo Coo Club. She walked in and I knew by my sense of too collective an intake of breath it was her. I kept my eyes averted—I could tell by everyone else's eyes where she was, what route she took to the bar—and I yanked Stella's arm and got us the hell out of there. But last night, last night it was different. I was sitting at a table by the door, facing the bar. Stella was talking to Vince Mansur. I don't know what he was up to, I wasn't paying much attention. Something stirred over my shoulder, someone coming in the door, and I turned absently, involuntarily, and there it was, right there, right in front of me, that ass not three feet from my face—I admit, Steve, my first impulse was to quickly close the distance, teeth clacking...or like a Jap bomber into one of our carriers, and probably with the same sense of assurance, that such a sacrifice, or a sacrifice to such an idol, could not but be rewarded in the afterlife—"

"For most there is no life after that."

"Which is why I held my ground. But my eyes, Steve, I could not avert my eyes. And it didn't take Stella long to pick up on that, but she couldn't take her eyes off either, nor could Vince. Luckily, not far from the bar, Veronica must've run into someone she knew, for this pulsatile feline stopped and stood still awhile—not exactly still, her nates rolled up and down as she shifted weight and that too was something to see, as you know. She wore blue jeans—or else she has blue skin, somewhat rugged. And a sweater that was too short by about half—in the front, not quite as short in the back for reasons obvious when she swiveled enough to draw the eye up to those uncratered volcanos, rising and pointing out, what, about 40 degrees from perpendicular?"

"That's about right."

"And it was chilly last night. She came in out of maybe 40 degrees—come to think of it there may be something in that correspondence...check Swedenborg, am I right?"

"I read Swedenborg in high school. There's nothing there."

"Anyway, those nipples like my thumbs, back down to that ass, there's that bare waist, and that back, the dimpling ravines on either side of the spine..."

"I know what she looks like."

"Even Stella could not keep her eyes off her body. It's impossible to exaggerate the sexual power of that woman."

"Yes it is. What about Vince?"

"He just sat there, a cobra tamed by the ghanoon, or whatever, utterly transfixed, speechless, impotent."

"She couldn't stand him. She said it wasn't worth her time to break him."

"So she's got her Albert Schweitzer side after all."

"Get to the catfight."

"The catfight…where to start…A prepared speech: Never have I been more uncertain that the abolition of private property would not achieve the collapse of hierarchy. Let's see…a crowded bar, a Friday night, she entered alone, and would only have to leave that way if she so chose. I had no erection. What does this erection signify? All those erections—like plants straining for the sun, fleshy heliotropic naifs. For me, I think it's hope for a better way to die. If I was only a little broader of chest, narrower of waist, darker of hair, chiseleder of features, stern of eye, mysterious like you, then maybe I could have walked right up to her—so long, Stella—placed my hands on her without a word, and tangoed her out the side door into the alley of our mutual demise."

"Mutual?"

"Maybe not. Now, you must be curious as to the identity of the other principal."

"Not Stella, I hope."

"No, Stella was transfixed elsewhere last night. I won't be coy any longer. It was Mitzie Skumsrud. So we have another ass, rumored to be unclad, or overdraped merely by dress. Rumor confirmed, though I have to say the many times I watched her stroll over the vents she was always wearing undies but for once or twice. Last night, no, no undies. That somewhat more slender, to a degree droopier, and to be fair three decades older, ass, was not confined by undergarment.

"But how did it start? By confluence of many accidents. I'll admit right here to a certain attraction I won't call perverse between Mitzie and I, which means I tend to keep an eye on her, and she me. The knowing glance—she's good at it, she's an old flirt. Of course, she knows I'm happy with my little Stella, and if there's anyone who understands such things it's the older woman in constant lust for a younger man. So what it amounts to is we give each other the occasional knowing glance, which is how I know that not five minutes before dona Slade showed up she was seated at the bar next to a rather handsome younger man, probably in his 30s. He had a kind face and a wide farmer back and it was clear he liked the old broad; there was a chemistry there—I don't mind saying I felt something this side of jealousy, a twinge of loss I think is the natural response to the knowledge that an act of mating will exclude you—it's instinct, and mean, I know...but at the same time I was happy for her. She was going to get laid and it wasn't going to be tawdry...she was holding her liquor well, she was inspired, she was—seizing a moment. All this of course from across the room, but I know I'm right and anyway subsequent events lend a degree of support...

"What I'm saying is by the time Veronica Slade reached the bar, having dismissed whoever it was wandered into her path, wandered solo up to the bar, rogue siren, her ass a ship's hull riveted by a tavern full of eyeballs—like that one?—by the time she got to the bar, Mitzie's conquest was gone to take a leak, leaving a single vacant stool—next to Mitzie Skumsrud."

"A script already written, as it were."

"As it happened. The bump Veronica gave to Mitzie's thigh, pointed toward the stool just vacated therefore in Veronica's way if she chose to approach the bar on the Skumsrud side of the stool, I suppose makes her the aggressor, though Mitzie fielded it with the aplomb of a pre-occupied demi-inamorata, stupored as she was in the repose granted fresh acquaintances by the much appreciated potty break: you need time to let things get heady, to reflect on your composure, especially to prepare the next smile: mysterious? insouciant? open? dangerous? threatening? sluttish? vulnerable?: that you'll greet him with.

"Mitzie glanced with instinctive forgiveness at Slade, then doubletook in the stunning nature of her beauty and mode of apparel, so that by the time Veronica could properly be said to have been oblivious of Mitzie's leg and response to getting it bumped, Mitzie was already alarmed at the thought of this great and terrible seductress her young farmboy conquest would confront when he returned from the privy, and, furthermore, aghast at that apprehension combined with the graceless prepossession with which dame Slade appropriated his stool.

"So: 'Excuse me,' Mitzie said, her venom concealed to the extent accumulated by the number of dinners she'd pulled off amongst wealthy people, if you follow."

"Not without extrapolation."

"So be it. Veronica's response was remarkable in more ways than most comments aspire to be: 'Don't trouble yourself, Grandma,' she said.

"And Mitzie's reply was suave enough: 'I'd trouble myself a lot less if you'd remove yourself from my friend's stool.'

"Now the Slade woman finally paid Mitzie some attention. Christ, how fast things happen! And how the wind of the wicked cuts both ways—past and future. I have no doubt that Veronica is only oblivious to the extent that her impervious steamrollering provokes no response. As soon as Mitzie challenged her, though, I mean, in a sense challenged her, she was quite conscious of having bumped Mitzie, as well as having misinterpreted Mitzie's sarcastic excuse me. And I have even less doubt that she very quickly honed in on Mitzie's fear, one of the primal-most amongst human females, that the bad woman will come and take her man away from the nest.

"And here already is where we choose favorites. Obviously, naturally. You got this skinny, aging bar skag, likes to flash in public, get drunk and humiliate her husband by way of humiliating herself, virtually cannot sustain any of life's momentum—for instance, just when you think she might at least get laid, she'll as often as not vomit in the poor bastard's lap, never deigns to buy a round despite being filthy rich, uses her money to advance her sexual cause alone—well, aside from that spent on necessary lubrication—yet fears being fiscally taken advantage of. You got her versus...the Vamp. The classic Vamp only bitchier. And far more beautiful. She tops Ava Gardner without a husky harumph. Or is that taking things too far? So who's side are you on? There's no clear favorite, though surely we'd like to see Veronica shed her clothes. I'll tell you who's side you choose, though I insist there is no clear favorite—if you're nine out of ten people you're on Slade's side, the side of youth and beauty. Intellectually, you might try to side with the underdog, but Skumsrud is rich and your gut tells you to pull for the champion filly. Of course, this is an urban phenomenon—if we were Italian peasants, say, we'd hate what we couldn't have and want it destroyed, a more fundamental response abstracted away from us by modern civilization, which is something to think quite a lot about, isn't it? Our pride becomes a shadow of our former self. Extrapolate from there and you get people who are without the sense of honor required to risk defeat rather than froth ringside at the boxing match that pits two brutes less and less like us as time goes on against each other—I give both last night's combatants more credit than the common man—"

"I'm not sure," Steve objected. "I'm not sure you can separate them, nor what happened, from the blighted modern man you refer to. I also object to the categorical Italian peasant example applied to the situation. The peasant can't have the money *or* the whore."

"Touché, or whatever's the Italian…Why don't you leave the record off now that it's over and you've made your demonic point."

Steve smirked into some imaginary alembic.

"Veronica Slade turned on Mitzie Skumsrud then, presenting her with a deliberate, manslaying smile, which of course meant something entirely different to Mitzie Skumsrud, to wit a display of immeasurable superiority. 'Why,' Slade proposed, 'don't we wait and see if your friend minds me sitting here? He may find there's room for both of us.'

"And as if that weren't enough, she aimed her charm at Ernest behind the bar: 'Ernest, I'll have a seltzer, and give this old broad something to calm her nerves.'

"Here your patience begins to reward. Mitzie couldn't have it both ways. As what passes hereabouts for a society woman she was obliged to swill liquor elsewhere and politely or stand accused of slumming. As such, she was forced by Veronica to choose quickly between the high and low roads. She's too high class to tolerate Miss Slade's precipitate bitchery, yet she's too much an inebriate regular to expect some appalled knight to come to her aid. She was on her own and it was time for her to act. She reached for her drink, said to Ernest, 'Never mind, Ernest, this one will do,' and splashed the half tumbler full of scotch right in Veronica's face. End of story. Only it was not end of story, for there is, these days, something afoul in the atmostrope.

"Now, Veronica was on Mitzie's right, and Mitzie used a backhand motion with her right hand to empty the glass. Veronica's response—I wouldn't call it immediate, for it was quicker than that—was a lefthand backhand across Mitzie's face. I suppose right there you have your class difference. At age 11 Mitzie was being tucked in by the maid, perhaps asking after Mommie's welfare, the headache she had when last seen the day before yesterday; while Veronica at age 11 was warning the babysitter to keep her mouth shut or she'd cut her nipples off, and make sure to lock the bedroom door on your way out lest Ma passes out before Pa.

"But bitterness can be a socioeconomic elevator—Mitzie rode it from the penthouse to the Coo Coo Club, whether for reasons of bad luck in marriage or something basic to her nature. Regardless, what she did next illustrates how comfortable she was becoming in her new station. She comes from a place where tossing a drink in someone's face marks the end of the scene, just like the little slap of the white glove used to before the upstarts got the upper hand, and here she tries it and gets a major league backhand across the cheek that immediately welted up finger lakes, nearly knocking her off her stool. No one could've blamed her had she said something condescending and feckless and stalked off to wait for her defeat to dissipate; or she could have arranged to have Slade arrested and raped by jailers—imagine the line. Instead, she returned to the issue of the stool, to wit: she knocked the dark Slade woman off hers. 'I suppose I deserved that,' clever, composed Mitzie said, and went into her swing just as Veronica untensed, went into her swing saying, 'Like you deserve this!', catching Slade with an earpopper, hitting her too high and inadvertently causing that particular type of headnumbing pain. The stool swiveled, Veronica's elbows, coming up in defense, surprise, or recovery—I don't know—her elbows bounced off the bar, her ass slid, gorgeous cataract, off the stool, and she landed on her knees, lucky she didn't bang her chin on the bar on the way down.

"Mitzie's mighty wallop brought time in the Club to a halt, which normally means nobody moved or said anything, but this time meant an actual halt in the progression of time, caused I am certain, by the suction that was the necessary inverse of Veronica's ear pop, or, if this is more appealing, the pop resounded, reverberated and redounded to a state of collective shock, leaving none to bear witness to the passing of time. Expectations cannot be obliterated without consequence.

"Certainly everyone there had their own reasons to refrain from interfering. We didn't all watch the way we like to watch a shark tear someone to pieces. It's possible, even, that most simply were too self-conscious. And there were surely those who considered it a matter of honor not to intervene. And those, too, whose motives were purely prurient. Not to mention various admixtures, my own beginning with prurience, passing through self-consciousness, and ending with honor. Or to be more fair to myself, you begin with my genuine interest in the way of things, that which has me mitzified…and then you can move on to prurience, which may account for most to some degree, though there is no denying that particularly patriotic laissez faire view of the world together with a provincial's appreciative awe of the magnitude of the event itself, staged unmagnanimously—yet proximitous—for *all*. Vince, to name one more, just hoped for a glimpse of Veronica Slade naked, and so falls entirely into the category prurient. Sissy was there, and both brothers, and I think there you get three different responses, perhaps, though I can't be sure: Nikkie not finding it interesting enough to disturb his billiards, Joe as yet unsure where his gallantry was called for, or he was late getting there, and Sissy perhaps intrigued in a particularly feminine way, a veteran of many an incipient barscrum herself, in fact, brained that fated night…

"Veronica got to her feet slowly, holding her hand to her ear, checking it once or twice for blood, like a young cowboy who'd just got knocked on his ass by his daddy. Mitzie stood in a grotesque bowlegged posture of preparedness, virtually snorting smoke out of her nose. The few patrons nearby quietly backed off to give the two more room. A barstool fell over, distracting no one. Who knows when the juke box had gone quiet. Everything was moving so slowly I took the opportunity to scan the crowd for Mitzie's conquest, and there he was, in the second or third row of horseshoed bystanders, a rather lascivious look on his face. I didn't like him so much anymore—you could see the plain unyielding mean of farm ethics on him. A guy like him could stomp a litter of barn cats with his boots while eating scrambled eggs off a skillet.

"The gloves were now off. No more snappy repartee. Only blood. I think Slade said as she lowered her head and prepared to charge, 'I'm going to steam your skinny ass,' nothing elaborate, nothing…demeaning even, a flatly stated threat, as believable as the only kind of promise that kind of woman believably makes. You, of course, know what I mean."

"She never threatened to kill me. She preferred a more matter of fact, 'I'll hurt you some day,' that sort of thing, which deep down you believe absolutely, and deeper down strive for. I would've been disappointed had it been otherwise. I would've had to find a different Last Woman."

"You're talking about the subconscious, one hopes."

"Absolutely not."

"So this alchemical turn was already in the making."

"It's ten years old, or thirty, depending how you look at it."

"Did you kill Evelyn Hartley?"

"No."

"All right, so it's not fair to say you've been driven to despair by a lovely woman, a femme fatale."

"I used her. I went out and found a femme fatale…and all I asked of her was that she be herself."

"She was in on it?"

"Not to her knowledge. I'm just another guy she sloughed off."

"What's this Last Woman business?"

"I can't tell you everything…I know you understand enough already…the point is it's useless to apply the brain to anything that does not involve survival, to that end all intellectual endeavor must have soteriological application—and I mean absolutely all, and towards an absolute salvation. You see, the beginning point of all wisdom is the acknowledgement of truth, followed by strict adherence to that truth. And to leap over several aspects of several millennia, we know that all religions have failed us, and science is more than my current expected lifetime from curing us of our nemesis death. Even the Hindus and Buddhists, while on the right *general* path, have failed. I've got thirty to forty years to succeed where they have failed—"

"Can I interrupt here?"

"You want to get back to your story? You have an appointment?"

"No, look, I don't think so, but do you think you're insane?"

"It could be that I'll have to be to succeed. But I think my motivations reflect as high a degree of sanity as you'll ever bear witness to."

"I agree. But tell me how the Last Woman will prevent my death."

"Not yours—maybe not even mine. And it could be that I've misfired. I would recommend my program to no one."

I was getting impatient.

"What program?"

"That's what I can't tell you. But I'll tell you this, if you've got another minute: modern man must recognize the obsolescence of reproduction, for it not only has outlived its usefulness, it carries within itself his death warrant. My starting point in my quest for personal salvation is the acceleration of the inevitable phases of my life."

"So you're through with sex."

"We all are, only I have realized it sooner. And I'm not just talking about the Hindu notion of the retention of semen—"

"*That* old notion."

"Every age has its representative man, its Hamlet, its Faust, its Lenin, who both rises above and illustrates his time. In fifty years modern man will be wandering lost in a wasteland of violence, Bakelite toys, and nihilistic sex. As usual, the most inhabitable of the cities—where the rate of atrophy is slower—will carry on oblivious to the degeneration of the species, rutting as if there were still something to rut for, sleepwalking into and out of defunct allegiances, nesting in abstractions... but the representative man will move about uncomfortably aware of his role as witness, as last messenger—mathematically the last possible, for there will be no one to deliver the message to...For him loneliness and isolation will be passé, he'll be beyond them, carry them within as fact like supernumerary organs, appendices, inoperable of course. For him each sexual encounter will be a step toward his final act, which he will accomplish without desperation..."

"What will that be?"

"That's up to him."

"Christ, you're a born anticlimax...Shall we go on then? Or have you lost interest in your anti-Eve?"

He nodded, and looked off toward the apocalypse he was already bored with.

"'I'm going to steam your skinny ass,' Veronica warned, as she began moving clockwise in on Mitzie, who obeyed the im-

provised laws of the dance, warily mirroring Veronica's movements. The two of them succeeded in making a full circle and
about another 107 degrees before Slade attacked, faking high
as she came on, ducking and driving her shoulder into Mitzie's
midsection, the thrust pinning Mitzie's back to the bar, while
Mitzie flailed like a woman at Veronica's back, unable to gain
force, leverage or position, unable to land a respectable blow.

"At this point the stupidest person in the bar—because the
prophet Steve wasn't there—the stupidest person in the bar
yells, 'Catfight!'

"Veronica maintained a grip around Mitzie's waist while
Mitzie's fists descended like virga furiously near her back. If she
let go the fists would no doubt pummel her head, but she was
unable to press her advantage. She hadn't thought it through.
As a tall, thin fellow I've never understood this approach, seen
so often in Westerns. Rather than trade wild roundhouses one
of the cowpokes dives at the other and they roll around on
the saloon floor. I've never understood it. I fear having my
natural advantage, my reach, effectively removed. Veronica
had done so, but now she was stuck. Mitzie's reach, though it
wasn't reaching, was still a factor. I wonder what Miss V was
thinking—they were deadlocked like that for a good ten or
twenty seconds, long enough for the crowd to press perceptibly
closer, for a few people to shift, for someone to snarl, 'Get out
of the way.' Both women exuded grunts. At one point Mitzie

lifted a leg—ah, a new weapon!—but she had to plant it again to maintain her balance, for in that instant Vero the hero nearly had her on the floor.

"Finally, as if she suddenly realized she was a lady and should therefore fight like one, Mitzie got a grip on Veronica's auburn locks and yanked savagely, eliciting a shrill shriek that seemed to be trying to formulate into 'Bitch!' Mitzie liked the sound so much she tried it again with the same result and more: Veronica finally freed her hands to strike and struck with a vengeance, clawing up and into Mitzie's cheek, drawing the blood we were longing for with one swipe. Mitzie released Veronica's hair and held her face Munch-screamwise and yowled like a mad monk.

"Veronica this time pressed her advantage, grabbing Mitzie's dress and whirling her to the floor, the front of the dress tearing open so that two lowslung rubbery bulbs, or bulbery rubs, could bobble to rest as Mitzie groaned on her back on a tavern floor.

"How far she'd fallen. Look at her, Steve, down there on the dirty floor of the Coo Coo Club like the wild daughter of a degenerate scion waiting for one of her brothers to come and collect her, eager to witness with her hangover Daddy's efforts to stall the scandal. If I thought it wasn't over I'd have gone to her like that brother, thrown my coat around her, escorted her out of there. But hell hath no fury like a broad tossed to a tavern floor so's that her dress tears and her tits flop out. Likewise hath hell no fury—"

"By the way, hell doesn't have fury."

"Right, Lucifer. It hasn't the fury of a woman used to getting her way having had her hair pulled, at least.

"O elegant brawling maven, how patient your revenge! How complex. Mitzie stunned at her feet, Veronica Slade turned to the bar mirror, turned back, looked down at the wealthy Madame Skumsrud, smirked, threw back her hair, adjusted the neck of her sweater, brushed her palms against her fiercely—fiercely!—triumphant breasts, stepped up to Mitzie, and swung her leg back to deliver a kick that Mitzie had time during Veronica's preening to prepare for, rolling away just in time, scrambling to her feet and lurching a nearly genuine punch into Veronica's mouth just as Veronica turned to receive the blow, which sent her windmilling backwards into a crowd that had the decency to part so she could plop onto her ass.

"Mitzie charged. Veronica stood. Mitzie kicked Veronica's knee. Veronica issued a phantom shriek—for the blow was glancing—and bent forward, Mitzie pulled at Veronica's sweater, a breast fell out without shame or tender feelings, a stout nipple errant and dark that made the men in the tavern gulp and hear themselves gulp...and sit (or stand) very still.

"The focus of the battle shifted to the sweater. Blinded by it, as Mitzie had it pulled over her head—a good streetfighter would have left it there and taken the opportunity to pummel Veronica's face with uppercuts—Veronica clutched the sweater and tried with a twisting motion to pull free. It was clear to me that the first one to relinquish the sweater would have the advantage, and I was puzzled that Veronica struggled so desperately to keep it on…"

"Artifice become near unconscious nature."

"I'll think that through later, but it sounds apt enough."

"Women like to decide for themselves when to take their clothes off."

"I'll remember that next time some dame is kicking my ass in the local. Mitzie finally released the sweater so as not to be swung around with the stronger Veronica, who fell to the floor from the force of the cyclonic motion, yet was nonetheless swung to the side, her hip bone colliding with the corner of a table. This time Veronica did not preen. Once the sweater was back roughly where it started, she rose from her knees, blood now dripping from her nose and smeared like a crazy woman's lipstick around her lips, and closed determinedly upon Mitzie, who stood gasping and holding her hip with both hands, her back hunched, her moans broken, as was what spell had had her entranced: She looked up, square in the middle of apperception granted her once this nightmarish ballet, to see herself from a face hovering in the crowd: 50-year-old Mitzie Skumsrud nee Sorenson, heir to a medical fortune, wife of a real estate fortune, mother of two girls off somewhere, one getting refined, the other fine-tuned, member of whatever clubs hadn't yet officially acted on her absenteeism, owner of and accomplished driver of the only white Rolls in western Wisconsin, graduate of Dartmouth with a degree in Geography, standing hunched and hip-holding, haplessly, exposed breastedly, watching the slow oncoming of the harpy sent to finish her off, for the descent into depravity had stalled one rung from bottom. Mitzie had the best view in the house, of the left hook Veronica delivered, the bones cratering her right eye socket, which lifted Mitzie's feet off the ground, sprawling her over the table she'd so recently met, yet which this time came to her aid in that it cradled her fall—she slid to the floor instead of falling in a heap—and the marauding Slade woman had to get around it to get at Mitzie, who was already sliding away like a landed crawdad.

"Yet Veronica reached her in time to land a hard kick to her rump, hard enough that Mitzie forgot about the pain in her eye and apparently got mad again, mad enough to turn into the next kick, bear it in her midsection, and catch the foot, pull up on it, and upend Veronica, who landed between tables. Mitzie scrabbled up her body and went at her hair again, pulling at both sides with the angly vigor of a skinny person.

"Here's where it became a true catfight. One of Mitzie's hands escaped with a clump of hair—a hard thing to watch, let me tell you—but Veronica sunk her teeth into the other hand, drawing blood and a scream and getting her face scratched for her triumph. The battle now was too closely fought for punches and kicks. The face-scratching got Mitzie her hand back, but begat scratches in kind—on the same cheek she'd already once had scratched—and within seconds each of the ladies lost further clumps of hair.

"It was an amazing scene. Thirty or forty people in the bar, absolutely still, not uttering a sound, and the two women bunched together like the proverbial doublebacked beast, nobody within six or ten feet of them. Suddenly, belatedly I'm sure, it almost seemed obscene to be watching. At least here is where it struck me. And I mean obscene in a different way, as if we were intruding on their intimacy—their movements so close, their grunts, moans, and cries so verily private…You know, when I'm in a fight or threatened with one, the first thing I take into consideration is the crowd. I'm thinking of the end of the fight, as in will somebody break it up before I get killed. Neither of the women had such concerns. It was attrition, a fight to the death, their entire focus on wounding or destroying the other. I'm not sure I'm even sure how they got up off the ground.

"Such scrumming ought to end with one of the two who's had enough asking the other who's had enough if she's had enough. The answer should be yes, the riposte should be same here, and they should part with thin unamiable dignities stretched thin as bat patagia but intact. Instead it was a bite perpetrated on Mitzie's neck. She pulled back with such involuntary force a bunch of her hair left her scalp and hung from Veronica's hand like cotton candy. Both were pained and startled, glad for the brief pause, and ready for the reprise. Mitzie stood without retreating and kicked Veronica, still sprawled, quite near her genital pouch. Veronica rolled and stood and advanced into the vigorous flailing mill of Mitzie's gangly arms, aiming her nails straight for Mitzie's pendulary chest sacs, succeeding in digging all ten tiny spades into the superfluous flesh, oblivious of the few light and glancing blows she was now safely inside of.

"We both know the female breast is as fickle and temperamental as the female herself, perhaps exceeding her in volatility. What is more sensitive than the pre-menstrual nipple? Yet so many women likes their tits manhandled, even bitten, at their estrousmost. In fact, it's one thing all women say well: You can be rough with them if you like. Bite them…harder. Pull my nipple—hard! Like this…That's my favorite, when they show you. I love to watch a woman handle her own breast, cupping it, pulling the nipple, squeezing it like a purring cat arranging its bed, squeezing it like a monkey popping a banana out of its skin, digging her own nails in, lifting it to her mouth and sucking her own nipple, lifting it to her own mouth and biting the nipple: see? Hard: a sort of mocking tribute to herself and her body, challenging you to try to please her the way she can please herself—Dig your nails into my breast. A classic, ancient love technique much extolled in Near Asian love poetry: the marks of the crescent moon on her breast, the moon marks of love on her pomegranates, as if he would peel her mango to reveal the swollen seed of her love…"

"Good god, Bobby. Next you'll be telling me how essentially ordinary are Veronica's breasts."

"How dare I would."

"All right. The point being that Mitzie had ten nails gouged into her breasts, which I imagine your ex-girlfriend thought would be the *coup de grace*. But Mitzie kept her composure, for reasons hinted at. She strikes me as the kind of broad who likes to be on the receiving end of a little rough stuff. Perhaps a means to sucker in the old dog when she can get him to bed, some secret sanctified paingiving. I wonder if the Skumsrud's have a butler. Can you imagine? I would like you to hurt me, Ronald.

"Or maybe it was simply alert adrenal glands, for she did not so much as cry out.

"Slade having tied herself up to no immediate avail, Skumsrud reached over her back and pulled up her sweater. The sweater again. Sensing that the battle was rapidly turning against her, Veronica enacted a clinch, bringing her teeth to bear on Mitzie's upper right chest without releasing the tits she still gripped. Mitzie jerked her upper body back, at the same time pulling the back of Veronica's sweater over her face. She had to jerk back a second time to detach herself from Veronica's teeth, which tore a bit of skin. One of Veronica's hands came free as well, waving blindly like an elephant trunk while Mitzie surged forward again to get hold of the sweater. The chest bite seemed to send Mitzie into a new level of rage. Her face was blotched and scratched and mean, her lips swollen and stretched over her teeth, her eyes lively with uncommon hatred. She got the back hem of the sweater over Veronica's head where it pinned itself against her face, thoroughly disabling her, leaving her open for a wild and solid left handheel slap to the temple, a blow that disturbed from deep within Veronica a guttural grunt and buckled her knees as several men in the bar gasped, and one of them, probably the idiot who had yelled catfight, moaned, 'Jesus.'

"That, effectively, was the end of it, the wealthy and cultivated Mitzie Skumsrud transported into a murderous frenzied hag, and avenging harpy herself. Granted, I was on her side, but isn't it amazing how the rich always come out on top? And especially against the climbers, which a broad like Veronica Slade has no choice but to be. At least in our bereft imaginations. Not that that was what this was all about, but look how it turned out. But I want to pause to defend myself a little, which is at least twice as bad as no defense, nonetheless a necessary expiation.

"It was an ugly scene, all right. Two humans tearing into each other like Johnny Reb and whoever the Union guy was, Abe Lincoln. Call it Korea on a small scale. And look how blood thirsty we were. I couldn't name the excitement—certainly it wasn't pure bloodlust. Nor all sexual. A lot of both, I'm sure.

But more than anything I'd call it penance, chance for a different reaction to boredom. Something spectacular as a bursting planet offered itself to us and we accepted. No one among us had the transcendent decency to step forward and proclaim: This is horrible, it must stop. And really that's the amazing thing, that there wasn't a single one. Otherwise I don't mind, Tavernus Maximus in full display, the lower depths, catfight at the Moulin Rouge, a little scuffle in the floating world, a cabaret brawl—decadent splendor enjoyed by all, no? But it leaves a bad feeling in my stomach, a little like after a public display of cowardice. Which maybe it was, all right, I'm a bit confused myself. There were moments when I lapsed out of my spectatorial enthusiasm and felt a little queasy, and I'm sure I wouldn't have let either of them get killed—though at any time if either of them had thought to grab a bottle and bust it on a table...indefensible, my position is indefensible, and I defend it as penance, to underscore my guilt. I got too much of a kick out of it, and I'm getting it now, too...stalling...

"The sweater came off with the slow inexorability of depraved revelation, Veronica Slade stunned, unresisting, Mitzie Skumsrud pulling the sweater off her extending arms in the posture of a jackal dragging a corpse into a ditch, and when she finally had it free in her hands, stumbling a step or two backwards, there on the polished grime and fresh stains of the tavern floor lay the sultriest woman in the city face down arms forward, torso twisted—

"'Look at that,'" some bewildered oaf said. Unnecessarily, for their utter nudity was too evidently the climax hoped for by all, and their nature remained, you still couldn't touch them and had they been tipped by sentient eyeballs there would have been no difference.

"Her birthmark—one imagines, perversely, a heart—just where the armpit began its scloff downward to her right breast—dark as the blood of stigmata, staring like the malicious open eye of a dead beast, announcing once and for all in its defeat that those caught by its spiteful, afflicted glare would thenceforth walk to their graves on shiftier sands...not all that bad a fate as fates go, no worse than harboring eyeballs where the nipples should be in a land lacking magical powers. No dwarves, no hunchbacks..."

"There's a dwarf at the brewery."

"Poisons the beer, no doubt, laces it with a monster's dreams. All right, I've seen him, but he certainly doesn't hold a position at the royal court. He isn't even allowed at the poker game. Anyway, my lament is false: Veronica Slade doesn't need any more powers than she already has, or had..."

"Nothing will change. Christ, you have to know a woman like her has her angry, sardonic moments, when she feels like revealing everything, whipping around to the crowd in the bar:

'Everybody get a good look? Can I drink in peace now, without your eyeballs climbing me like parasites?'"

"She tell you that?"

"Some knowledge can't be passed on."

"Just tell me that much."

"Suffice it to say that to the rest of you she is human."

"All right. But her bare breasts certainly held the attention of the crowd—all but Mitzie Skumsrud, who was the last to give a rat's ass. She had stumbled back, and now that she had the sweater in her hands she must have felt as if that alone ended the battle, mythological parallels obvious and many. Or call it capture the flag. But she soon gathered her wits and tossed the thing aside, knocking a mug off the table, for some beer must be spilt, the crash breaking a rather turbid silence. She had every reason to suspect from experience of the previous ten minutes (I estimate) a vicious attack, so I don't think she can be faulted for what she did next, though it was the most vicious event of the entire sequence. Veronica was still dazed, and was just lifting her head, beginning to contract in preparation to rise, when Mitzie landed a kick along the left side of her face. I think you'll know what I mean when I say: sickening onomatopoeia. It wasn't quite a thud. Its emotional essence was squishier than that. Obviously there was the potential removal of an eye, not to extend an obsession, to account for this. Then there's the broken teeth that might have been—yet it was to a degree a glancing blow that to an exhausted and virtually ruined Veronica Slade, who had to have held somewhere in her mind the knowledge that her lack of real secrets, her—back to correspondence—her oblatery, her near symmetry, the nothing mysterious that eliminated right then and there the effect she must have at least taken some pleasure or pride in would of necessity take a leave of absence. She slumped her head right back to the floor.

"Mitize's rage was visibly subsiding now. She half-heartedly circled her victim, giving some thought to delivering another kick, when she herself stopped and stood gaping, bent a little forward at the waist, having entirely forgotten that her own tits were hanging out, that her face was scratched up, her lips bleeding. I don't know what she saw down there, but she stared for a good ten seconds, and quite suddenly pulled a leg back, apparently intent on a next mighty kick—for Mitzie there would be no epiphanic break in the exoteric tavernity, when the Judge, who had walked in just a second before, saw Mitzie Skumsrud no less, standing over a topless woman, her tits hanging out, a truly sordid scene, which he brought to an end: '**Mrs. Skumsrud**,' he said, stopping her leg just in time. He paid no mind to anyone else in the bar, not even Veronica—he might at least have checked her pulse, for she wasn't moving. He strode across the floor, directly up to Mitzie, somehow making a silent crowd even more silent—what elegant and bizarre authority erupted onto that squalid scene—and you may as well throw refinement in there too, and class, that enormous lawgiver in his three-piece suit that always looks on him rather like seven or eight well-fitted pieces. '**Mrs. Skumsrud**,' he said, walked up to her, put his arm around her, said, '**It is time to leave**,' and walked her out of there, Mitzie looking up into his stoic granite face the whole time like a ravaged, starving cherubim.

"You could've heard an ant fart after they left. We had no choice but to gape at our own shame in the form of Veronica Slade slowly lifting herself from the floor, her two magnificent breasts that I am sure absolutely everyone in there wished were elsewhere, rising oblivious, grotesquely out of place, almost gauche, twin faux pas...

"Christ...She stood full and erect—Homo erectus, by god, and the rest of us be damned: we didn't know what to do. Her face bloodied, swollen, misshapen, one evident bald spot, her eyes surprisingly—thankfully—aglint with defiance, she faced an audience of weak fools, faced us down—we'd feasted on her and she knew by her own survival we would come out of it hungry. She would have hated us all, but we were not worthy. Now you understand *beneath contempt*. I could see her ascending to the gods, to return and destroy our city...But not really, for she was among us still, a long way from exhausting the profane; she could still be queen, if this was all there was for subjects.

"'Somebody get me my goddamn sweater,' she said with a penetrating fluency of scorn.

"Ernest scurried around the bar and plucked it from the floor without pausing, like a polo player bending sideways off his horse. Veronica Slade wasn't impressed enough to look at him. She pulled her sweater on, hesitating once her eyes were through the neck hole, utilizing the sweater as a veil while she seared the crowd one last time with her Mediterranean eyes, which by nature harbor ancient curses."

So I long to expose my own sacs of dirty secrets, my areolas of weakness, my titsacs filled with the detritus of my past good deeds, souring, sagging toward the grave. So I cannot trust what I thought I saw, a tear slinking to the horizon of Steve's eye, and in the other the last mote of his fear.

Marla Rothgert

Want to hear my black sonnet? Here's my black sonnet. Listen to my black sonnet, you anus: Nightblind and furious scrabbling shed from me the smallest lies that I may tunnel down unfettered slick and grieving down to blind the long defile of silent dead retrieve of these most sullen skulls the three who least remember me nor lie and know the darkest lie these three then to return with me to lie only the darkest lie and lead me darker still to those who die!

Oh, nice.

How nice.

One-Arm Buzzy, Spring, 1954

I heard it from that Spangler kid making a morning delivery and it really burned my stump. I wasn't surprised Bobby never mentioned it to me, he was too ashamed. He knew if I'd been there it wouldn't of lasted ten seconds.

But before you castigate him completely you have to know Bobby, he had his sensitive side. He dropped by the station about when I was closing, he had the day off, he dropped by and I could tell he dropped by specifically for me to tear him a new rectal. Spring was an absolute when you could feel it at night, when you don't even think about it and just take your beers out beside the building and tilt the chair back 'gainst the wall and watch the traffic.

Ever had the feeling that somehow gravity and the urge to flight came to sudden pause right there in your very lap so it was up to you to keep the thing going? You recognize it by the weightless waft of wisdom, the ease of generation without humility or the need for humility. I don't even know what I'm getting at—or I don't know how. Whichever.

The thing about Veronica Slade was that sure she was a sexy dame, but Bobby liked to make more of things sometimes, for the fun of it, maybe, though I suspect sometimes he needed to and don't ask me why or what that means. Whenever she came to the station, Bobby refused to service her car, I had to do it, that Sirens thing he come up with. But even that was only a game of some kind, to do with his crazy talk about nipples, trapped mother in father's bra of civilization he put it one time if I remember right, or a hundred if not. He never figured me for understanding such broad talk, but I get more than he thinks. Now enough was enough and he knew it. We were quiet for a long time, near done with our beers, when I said, "You know, Bobby?" He didn't look at me, just moved his head unperceptively. "The day after Evelyn got took you and Stella stayed home and we never talked about it but I was like almost everybody in town that day, or what seemed like everybody in town, down to the crime scene volunteering for search parties. I ended up in the bean fields most of the day, and who beside me most of the time but Veronica Slade. I couldn't tell you what we talked about, Bobby, walking off out of the last of the city to the bean fields to the bluff, the woods at the foot of the bluff—Christ, the shit you find in the middle of nowhere—"

"Detritus."

"Bless you."

"Mention it."

"What about last night? Stella there?"

"She was home studying."

"Your ass sucks buttermilk."

"My ass sucks buttermilk? Where do you get that crap?"

"From you, if I remember right."

And you couldn't help but rise above the fields and the houses and look down at what we all were in our thousands, scrabblers, like ants, scrabblers rootin' about, each and every one of us thinking like a purposed human but from up there looking down we was just scrabblers with no more meaning than ants 'cept for Evelyn's brother heroic through the sewers coming out like a miner with women's undergarments instead of one them lamp helmets. Someone, I think it was one a them Turner boys, said he had about five bras and who knew how many panties...

I bet you can't find a single square acre in the city without no condom or beer can...

"I don't remember a single thing we said that day, Bobby, but you know we known each other her whole life, practically neighbors, always on a conversational basis if we were stuck alone together, no matter I'm older. That day we was just two people making the necessary gesture that wouldn't change nothing but we knew like everybody seemed to that if enough people made that gesture...well something unspeakable would be replied to with some kind of vague speaking...Thing is you don't think about the likely futility of it at the time, you just have to add to the number so the city can make something like a show of strength to the futility..."

"You're losing me, Buzzy. I mean that's true poetry, but I'm not sure I foller your intentions." But his voice wasn't smartass Bobby, and I saw his eye was wet.

"So what about Veronica Slade?"

Scratch that. If his eyes was wet it was the breeze.

"Let me get two more."

Just the breeze in the hackberries...

"Even if you know it, that's the point, I guess."

"Sure enough, Buzz: but I tell you I was grateful Stella was in no shape to get out that day. I wanted no part of it. I still don't."

"What do you mean?"

"Think about it: You can't think about it."

I wasn't sure what he was getting at.

"What a night," he said, bringing his chair forward and eyeballing his bottle like what he had to say was swimming in there.

"Can't you see it, Buzz?"

I looked at the bottle, like now I thought it was in there.

"What's that, Bob?"

I'd thought it was safe to return my thinker to more typical thinking.

"It's a whole season's pass't...just like the rush of the water at the end of its draining, things are speeding up to swowl away what you can't think about."

And so then there were these times I had no idea what to make of it...

Yeah, Bobby. He went quiet then, and in a little while he was smiling, it was such a beautiful spring evening. What little he had, he had all he ever wanted. The past and future could disappear that sudden for him. I knew by then he wasn't going to mention the Veglan thing and I knew why, too. I wish I could've told him I knew and I wish I could have told him I was glad I didn't have to bear it with him.

Bobby, Spring, 1954

I guess I'd been feeding Stella just enough that the gingham was stretching at the hips and the torso under the breasts. I loved her in that dress, that little waitress dress that seemed like it was perpetually restraining or failing to restrain that tensile, felinely woman inside it, my pussy cat. Be bop, Stella, a *lula*, baby. If she wanted, I decided, I'd even dance with her. The way to rid one's self of a bad night or a bad week, short of holy penance, is to have a good night or a good week, and how many times with Stella did we cram the ground meat of a great week into the sausage skin of a single night? If only she weren't so goddamn excited about the whole thing, if only her body would stick to the point, if only her excitement were limited to Gene Vincent and his goddamn Blue Caps and did not extend to the anticipation of yet another scene, yet more blood, and this time with her own gladiator on public display. Not that she uttered a word about it, she didn't have to, everybody else was. The girls couldn't leave her alone. Randy Shifter herself dropped by Stella's house to talk about it. Molly Bott called wanting to know when we were going to be there.

Read: Are he and Vic going to fight before or after the show? Will they go across the street behind the gas station or will Bobby pull something dirty like knifing Vic on the dance floor? Will Bobby knife Vic in the ass like a Turk? Gaby Mansur, that sleek hussy, even called me, at my place.

"Is Stella going to let you go to the concert?" she asked.

"I don't know, minxy, I haven't applied yet."

"You know you don't stand a chance, don't you? You pull a knife on Vic and you're steamed."

"What if I toss a bouquet of roses at his feet?"

"The only chance you got is to leave town."

"Okay, Gaboony baboony, I'll leave town."

"He's going to kill you."

Click.

Stella never said a word about it, not to me, my proud little whippet. We walked all the way from my place, all the way downtown, all the way down the causeway, her little hips pumping lustily, giving my proprietary palm a wild ride. At the bridge over the La Crosse River one of us—you couldn't tell—got the idea to stop and kiss. And she was upon me like a country rassler, all wet and full and damp and soft and strong and damn near knocking me over the rail. I put her hand on my little pumper, hard as steel, and asked her, "You want to just go home?"

She laughed away my silly idea, sliding her hand over to the equally hard pocket knife to reassure herself. She kissed me again, but my ardor had already begun to wane. Onward march to the Avalon.

A car filled with the grand and loose wisdom of youth cruised by, arms flailing at us, dumblipped mouths hooting at us. Probably they weren't on either side, they were just headed for the shows.

Oh spring wind blowing everybody no good, a cool spring wind roughing our hair, tickling us inside our clothes, a spring wind that bode a frigid autumnal night, a good night for blood to spill into and congeal. Halfway down the causeway we could already see crowds milling, groups of two or three or, as we got closer, seven or more, and by the time we got to the Avalon parking lot they no longer looked up and looked down again, they looked and kept looking, they watched. De facto, it was like a boxer making for the ring.

One wondered where that other boxer might be.

One wondered if he would sneak up and knife one in that ass like a Turk.

Not far from there, in fact no more than a broken skull's toss, there'd been a magnificent gang fight around the turn of the century. All the Lebanese and Syrian immigrants, all those Wakeens and Mansurs and Markoses and the like, button folk or something—from river shells or something—some odd reason in La Crosse, they were ghettoed up there on the near north side and one night it all exploded into a fracas, hundreds of knife-wielding, bat-swinging, irate fighters. If I remember correctly only a couple were killed. It seems a miracle.

We went right into the joint and up to the bar. I usually like the mezzanine, but it could've been construed as an evasive maneuver. I also like to get drunk quick at shows, but that didn't seem a good idea either.

My greatest fear was that we'd have to endure a local band choking their lutes and banging their garbage can lids before the headliners started, but to my everlasting gratitude that wasn't the case. A string of Louis Prima songs was played instead.

Buona sera, senorina, kiss me goodnight

Stella and I sat at a small round table and waited for one of the shows to erupt. I guess all my friends were too old for this Gene Vincent business. I didn't ask Buzzy to come, because he would have, and that would have put him in the thick of it along with me. He heard about it, though.

"What's this Veglan business?" he had asked me a couple days before, I think the day Hopkins went berserk.

"Those are called rumors, Buzzy. There's nothing to it."

He gave me a big smile. "Okay," he said, and went off with a wrench.

And of course Steve would have come with a gun if I had asked, but he was a fatalist, and would have to be asked. I didn't ask.

So there we sat, Stella and I in our love bubble, our beers in front of us, and our hands on each other's thighs, and all her friends avoiding us, waiting, letting it all play the way it was going to play.

Barmitzvahed again

I suppose Gene hit the stage nine o'clock or so. I'll give him this much—he's a dynamo. Stella nearly leapt off her seat when she first saw him in person, and she got all trembly when the song started.

"You want to dance?" I asked her.

She looked around the place quick before answering.

"Let's just listen to the first one," she said.

The first one was a wild piece called 'Catman'. I kind of liked it.

Catman's a comin' and you better look out
Catman's a comin' runnin' about
Catman's a comin' lookin' for a girl
You better hide your sister, man

C is for the crazy hairdo that he wears
A is for the arm that he'll stick around your waist
T is for the taste of the lips belong to you

Catman
CATMAN!

Stella was wriggling like an eel in her seat.

Yeah! Get it!
Go!

He was a dynamic performer all right.

M is for the mean things that this mean man does
A is for all the hearts he has ever broke
N is for names of the list you may be on

"Catman," I said to Stella.

Catman.
CATMAN!

"Catman," she replied.

Rock!

Catman lookin' for a woman all day long
A better watch out because I feel he's in your midst
A better watch out or you gonna be kissed
A better watch out because I feel he's in your midst

Catman
CATMAN!

Yap!

There was a surprise ending:

Better watch out because a I'm the catman

Catman...

A slow song started, initiated by a guitar solo, and I could feel the tides pulling toward Vic Veglan, whom I gauged to be about fifteen feet behind me, on the edge of the dance floor, and I could already see the way he stood apart from everybody else with his arms across his chest, waiting for me.

"I better get this over with," I told Stella.

She knew what I meant.

"Be careful," she said, rising to accompany me.

The band kept playing, but half of everybody was watching me weave through the field of tables up to Vic Veglan.

"Hello, Victor," I said.

He wasn't there for small talk.

"Let's go across the street," he said, meaning out of the Avalon and across the street behind the gas station.

"I'm not going across the street, Victor."

"Don't call me Victor."

"Mr. Veglan, if we go ahead with this somebody is going to get hurt very badly, and I don't want that to happen."

I wished I couldn't feel Stella's surprise the way I felt it. She stepped away to look at me.

"You mean you're chicken," Veglan said.

"If that's what it takes to call it off."

"You flap your big goddamn lips and now you're backing out like a goddamn woman."

Gene started singing a love song, but I doubt anybody standing near me was listening.

"Or a little girl, what have you."

He stepped toward me and grabbed my shirt and pulled me close enough I could smell his aftershave. I kept my hands to my side, out of my pocket.

Through gritted teeth he said, "You're not getting out of it that easy. You're a wise ass, and tonight I'm going to teach you a lesson, steam you pro bono."

I didn't expect *that* kind of challenge. Pro bono. Had he accidently threatened me with elegance? I kept a straight face.

"You go. I'm staying. Or you stay, and I'll go."

I looked over to Stella, who was a few feet farther away, tears starting in her eyes.

Veglan saw where I was looking. Tears started popping out.

"Here's your big shot," he said with raw contempt, releasing me. "Go ahead, Stel, I'll let you take him out of here. Only I ever see him where there ain't a crowd, he's not so lucky. Go ahead, take your little sister out of here."

I sort of knew what was coming.

"Let's go, Stella," I said.

I think Gene Vincent was singing about a broken heart or something real sad like that.

She shook her head a little—as implacable as *no* can be.

I could be implacable, too.

I turned and walked out of there, half expecting to get jumped out in the fresh air, but not expecting the bushwhacker would be Gabie Mansur, who came running up to me, breathless with some silly notion of triumph.

"I'll take you away, Bobby," she said, rife with entendre, "I got my dad's car."

Stella, Oct. 24, 1953

Probably we were the last people in the city to find out. It was almost midnight when this guy I never met, Joe Kneifl, the guy from Florida, came in and said he heard it on the news. I was only half paying attention, I was a little drunk, and there was that hilarious thing with the judge, and Bobby had his hands all over me, and I wanted him pretty bad myself, and somehow the words came at me like little waves, from one end of a sea to another, and the little whitecap on top of the wave was Evelyn Hartley, the name being carried to me like a wave until it finally hit me what it was all about, that Evelyn Hartley had been attacked and kidnapped and there was blood everywhere and she was dead, and who'd've thought hard little Stella could get so upset over something like that but I screamed and screamed and everybody was looking at me, and Bobby came up and didn't put his hand over my mouth, he just held me there next to the bar and let me scream. It had all been so beautiful up to then, so very grand and beautiful a night. And Bobby took me home and waited 'til he found out it was what I wanted to make love to me, and he was never more gentle than that, never so slow, and he kissed my head like I was his little girl, again and again and all over he kissed my head like I was his little girl, he kissed my head without going shh, it's going to be all right, he just kissed my head and made love to me as slow as can be, and he went on and on until the sun came up, somehow he knew I would be all right if the sun came up.

Bobby, Spring, 1954

The elements eternal: the spring wind unchilled in a convertible with a frisky dame by my side and out-of-town liquor in my veins and all that's necessary to refresh a life gone inexplicably stale, as if a lollipop turned into the barrel of a gun, but O spring night chill, and O good whisky, and O the bad girl, she let me drive, back down toward Irish Hill, and the headlights were infinite, fading into the black that nightly ate the green hills, her olive oil kisses, the purr of a good engine, and the warmth of her chilly body rubbing up to me, the headlights inching down a horizon of their own making, and the moon oblate above, and the moon straight ahead, my lights converging in the mouth of the dark and beyond a single moon weaving toward us, emerging from the mouth of the dark a weaving moon: O spring night, O drunken love, O hard young breasts under the one moon and the other coming towards us, at the top of the hill, this planetary convergence in the infinite space of seconds, and a last smile, a love of spring and whisky and women and five dollars' worth of irony: He's going to kill someone someday.

Todd Mills

Go away now.

"Go away now."

Little things can be so heavy. And heavy things flimsy.

Pneumatics crisp.

"'Because that's what he wanted.'"

That's what he wanted.

What he wanted.

"Shut the door. Leave me for a while."

Leave me for a while.

Thanks to the generous support of our founding Go Fund Me campaign supporters, including Robert Armagost and the Maintenance Ends Founding Board of Supporters: Lisa Taggart, Trenton Lee Stewart, Sesshu Foster, Prasenjit Gupta, Mary O'Connell, Diane Hinton Perry and Stefene Russell.

Special thanks to Steve Semken of
Ice Cube Press, and Todd Kimm.

RICK HARSCH appeared on the American literary scene in 1997 with the cult classic *The Driftless Zone*, followed by *Billy Verite* and *Sleep of the Aborigines* (all Steerforth Press) to form "The Driftless Trilogy."

Born and bred in the Midwest, Harsch received degrees in sociology and history from UW La Crosse. Later he attended the Iowa Writers' Workshop, soon winning a Michener/Copernicus award for *Billy Verite*. In 2001, he migrated to the Slovene coastal city of Izola, where he still lives with his wife and two children.

Rick is also author of *Arjun and the Good Snake* (2011, Amalietti & Amalietti; 2018, River Boat Books), *Wandering Stone: The Streets of Old Izola* (2017, Mandrac Press), and *Skulls of Istria* (2018, River Boat Books).

MAINTENANCE ENDS is a Midwest-centric press dedicated to bringing fresh, off-center voices into print.

Maintenance Ends begins with the notion of exploring and discovering what lies beyond the path of the familiar. In that spirit, we aim to expand the notion of that most underestimated of safe zones, the Midwest.

As an imprint of the respected regional publisher, Ice Cube Press, LLC, Maintenance Ends is devoted to emerging and overlooked literary works of the Midwest. We present works of the Midwest by Midwesterners (and not), drifters, decoys or anyone whose work lays claim to the territory while demonstrating the elasticity of its boundaries. We regard no work as too experimental, too complex; no genre as out of bounds.